# WAIT FOR SIGNS

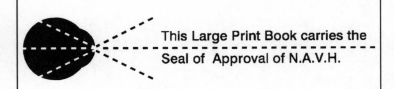

This Large Print Book carries the
Seal of Approval of N.A.V.H.

# WAIT FOR SIGNS

## TWELVE LONGMIRE STORIES

# CRAIG JOHNSON

**THORNDIKE PRESS**

*A part of Gale, Cengage Learning*

GALE
CENGAGE Learning·

Farmington Hills, Mich • San Francisco • New York • Waterville, Maine
Meriden, Conn • Mason, Ohio • Chicago

**GALE**
CENGAGE Learning·

**LIBRARY OF CONGRESS CATALOGING-IN-PUBLICATION DATA**

Johnson, Craig, 1961–
 [Short stories. Selections]
 Wait for signs : twelve Longmire stories / by Craig Johnson. — Large print edition.
 pages ; cm. — (Thorndike Press large print mystery)
 ISBN 978-1-4104-7532-9 (hardcover) — ISBN 1-4104-7532-8 (hardcover)
 1. Longmire, Walt (Fictitious character)—Fiction. 2. Sheriffs—Wyoming—Fiction. 3. Large type books. I. Johnson, Craig, 1961– Old Indian trick. II. Title.
 PS3610.O325A6 2014b
 813'.6—dc23                    2014035990

Published in 2015 by arrangement with Viking, a member of Penguin Group (USA) LLC, a Penguin Random House Company

Printed in the United States of America
1 2 3 4 5 6 7 19 18 17 16 15

For Eric Boss, Westerner,
gentleman, and
book rep of the first order.

"Too often I would hear men boast of the miles covered that day, rarely of what they had seen."

— LOUIS L'AMOUR

# ACKNOWLEDGMENTS

After I was fortunate enough to win the *Cowboys & Indians* Tony Hillerman Award with "Old Indian Trick," the first story in this collection and the first short story I had ever written, I got the bright idea that I'd send it to the folks who subscribed to my newsletter as a free gift for the holidays. On Christmas Eve, about ten years ago, I fired the story off at 11:59 Mountain Standard Time. I didn't really know what I was getting into until the following November when readers began asking me when I was planning on sending out this year's holiday tale, and as the communications began piling up, I rapidly figured out that I'd created a monster.

Knuckling down, I wrote another story and discovered that I actually enjoyed the process and the format, because it gave me the opportunity to address the small points in Walt's life that were pivotal but not appropriate for an entire novel. They run from twelve to forty pages — some are mysteries, some have mysterious elements, and others are no mystery at all, just glimpses into Walt's life.

People have often asked me if I have any intentions of killing Walt off someday, and I have to admit that I'm somewhat taken aback by the question. Never say never, but the greatest insurance that I'll not do that is the character of the man himself. Walt is kind, decent, caring — and I just like him and hope you will, too.

There's another group of people I'll never kill off, starting with actor, director, writer, and friend extraordinaire, Lou Diamond Phillips, and actor and big-dog sheriff, Robert Taylor. The adventure of having my novels adapted into the A&E television series has been a joyful affair, mostly due to the newfound friendships with the cast, the producers, and the crew, and to you, the new readers, but especially due to Lou and Rob. As only one example of the kindness and generosity of the men, I was asked to deliver the commencement speech on the Northern Cheyenne Reservation, and wrote the words, but then discovered that I was going to be on a book tour and couldn't attend. Lou jumped on a plane from Santa

10

Fe where he was filming *Longmire,* flew to Montana, and delivered the speech for me, much to the thrill of the Lame Deer High School graduating class and the Northern Cheyenne Nation. The man is a scholar and a gentleman on horseback, and I thank him for his generosity of spirit.

Gail Hochman, the agent above all agents and head ramrod to this wayward maverick, was instrumental in making the Longmire books and television series possible. Never without a kind or enthusiastic word, Gail was the only agent who would take on my first novel, *The Cold Dish* — little did I know, she was also the absolute best.

Kathryn Court is my wagon boss, the cowgirl errant who stands between me and a harmful word. Her constant and personal attention has made me and the series what we are today.

Ben Petrone has been a friend, confidant, and riding partner, along with Angela Messina, Scott Cohen, Maureen Donnelly, Lindsey Schwoeri, and Carolyn Coleburn.

Marianne Merola has kept a hard eye on the manifest and loaded these twelve dogies to parts unknown and languages unspoken by yours truly.

Here's also to those two cattle barons past, Tony Hillerman and Robert B. Parker, for looking out the window of the dining car and giving a cowboy from a town of twenty-five a leg up in making the big time.

And to Michael Crutchley and Chet Carlson, the railroad bulls who kept us on the level, and to Mike and Susie Terry, the original owners of the Divorce Horse. Thanks to Judy Slack and the Wyoming Room of the Sheridan Fulmer Library and the indomitable Vic Garber for all those marvelous stories that we listened to while those steel wheels rumbled on through the night. Thanks to the Teton Raptor Center for the phalanx of owls that flew along above us, and to Marcus Red Thunder for holding the flaming arrows at bay — except for Judy, the flaming arrow that gets through and pierces my heart every time.

# CONTENTS

# INTRODUCTION

Tightrope. It's not just a Clint Eastwood movie, or a circus performer's next trick. It's that thing upon which great mystery writers must boldly but carefully tread, precariously balancing the unwieldy burdens of plot, character, and setting, all the while enticing us to enjoy the journey and marvel at the view. Each step is carefully placed so as to stay one chess move ahead of the savvy readers — who, try as they might, should not be able to see the ultimate destination until their literary guide is good and ready to show them — but never to lose them. One misstep and the entire entourage tumbles into the abyss. Now, try doing it in cowboy boots, and you'll begin to comprehend the amazing feat that is each of Craig Johnson's Longmire mysteries.

I have the great honor of bringing one of his unforgettable characters, Henry Standing Bear, into the corporeal world — otherwise known as your TV — on A&E's *Long-mire.* Having read all of the Longmire books to date, I was understandably intimidated by the prospect. The Bear is so vividly drawn, both inside and out, that he virtually leaps from the page and into the reader's imagination. Preparing for the part, I kept thinking of the actor Will Sampson from the classic film *One Flew Over the Cuckoo's Nest,* and how beautifully he'd risen to the challenge of bringing Ken Kesey's Chief Bromden to life. Fittingly, it was a Samp-sonlike struggle to immerse myself into the role. Standing Bear's stature, both in height and philosophy, seemed so enormous that I quailed at the thought of filling his majestic moccasins — especially in the eyes of the man who had formed him from the Absa-roka clay, whom I'd be meeting before shooting began. Trust me when I say it's never easy to meet your creator.

I'd had the opportunity to meet the author of a literary character I was attempting to portray only once before. The year was 1991. The film was *The Dark Wind,* and I was playing Jim Chee, the iconic Navajo tribal police sergeant created by the great Tony Hillerman. Mr. Hillerman was warm, gracious, and more than magnanimous. Stately, even. He said I resembled Jim Chee as he'd always imagined him. Since he didn't comment on my acting, I took this comment as his tacit approval of my performance. Though my encounter with Mr. Hillerman was nothing but positive, it only made me more respectful of the genius it takes to create a character beloved by millions. So it was not without a little trepidation that I looked forward to meeting the rightful heir to Mr. Hillerman's literary legacy.

Fortunately for me, Craig Johnson not only inherited the mantle of literary genius from Tony Hillerman, but was also bequeathed his grace, warmth, and generosity. Now, sans the photo that graces the back flap of Craig's books, many a gentle reader could be forgiven for imagining that Craig Johnson might look like the weathered but erudite offspring of Louis L'Amour and Sir Arthur Conan Doyle. Not so much. The unassuming and open-faced man whom I met while filming the *Longmire* pilot was more evocative of the helpful clerk at your local Feed-and-Tack store who would gladly throw in a truckload of alfalfa if you would just purchase that beautiful hand-tooled saddle. (Okay, I wrote that last bit just to make Craig and his wife, Judy, laugh.) Still, Craig Johnson is not what you might expect . . . and yet he is everything you might expect. He is a man of letters and a man of his word. A laureate with a lariat, if you will. In short, Craig is the spring that feeds the very deep well that is Walt Longmire.

Not all of the short stories in this collection can be classified as mysteries, although there is a generous enough serving of plot thickeners to satisfy any attentive reader's appetite. The stories, taken together, remind me of the stained-glass windows in church that become an adolescent Walt's primary focus in "Slick-Tongued Devil." Each story forms a small but integral part of the bigger picture, a piece of the mosaic that we, Craig's faithful readers, have come to know as the world of Absaroka County and Walt Longmire. Each is imbued with its own unique color and illumination and can be considered a gem in its own right.

It occurs to me, too — though I've never actually ridden a horse with him — that Craig Johnson knows how to pack a saddle-bag. These stories are bulging with the western wit, warmth, and hard-won wisdom we've come to expect from his long-form fiction. He continues to make me laugh out loud at the most inopportune times. And yet it is Craig's hand with humanity, his empathy and compassion, that leaves the most lasting impression. I have often found myself rereading his sentences simply to absorb a profound truth that he's managed to convey with an economy and specificity Hemingway would admire. Craig paints the landscape of Absaroka County masterfully, inviting the reader to share his reverence for nature, and yet it is in his role as a guide to human nature where he is most intuitive. There is a resonant melancholy that blows in the breeze of Absaroka and occasionally ruffles Walt's unkempt hair. It whispers in the ear of the reader. It makes us feel. It makes us think. It makes us reflect on our own place in this vast wilderness. This is what art, in any of its forms, is supposed to do.

So as you read these newly collected entries into the Absaroka lore, and you find yourself on a lonely stretch of Wyoming highway or on a windswept, snow-covered plain, you might want to look up. The sky above Absaroka is often turbulent and indiscernible. But there are those times when it is clear. So crisp and blue and pristine that it might bring a tear to your eye. At those times, you might see Craig. Still up there on that tightrope. Still scanning the landscape like Henry Standing Bear's owls. Still maintaining that delicate balance between plot and profundity as he makes his away across.

And still wearing his cowboy boots.

— LOU DIAMOND PHILLIPS

# OLD INDIAN TRICK

It's hard to argue with an old Indian or his tricks.

I was driving Lonnie Little Bird up to Billings for an evening diabetes checkup at Deaconess Hospital when we pulled into the Blue Cow Café, on the Crow Reservation just off I-90, for some supper. The Blue Cow had been a restaurant longer than it'd been a casino; its MONTANA BREAKFAST! SERVED ALL DAY! AS FEATURED IN READER'S DIGEST! consisted of a half pound of bacon, four jumbo eggs, twelve pancakes, three-quarters of a pound of hash browns, a pint of orange juice, and endless coffee — a western epic, well known across the high plains.

We had gotten a late start — the sun was already sinking over the rolling hills of the Little Big Horn country and was casting surrealistic shadows against the one-ton hay bales of the Indian ranchers. It was September and, with the sporadic rain of a cool August, it looked like everybody was going to get a third cutting.

We rolled the windows half down and made Dog stay in the truck. I lifted Lonnie, placed the legless man in his wheelchair, and rolled him in. He smiled at the remains of the day and picked up a free *Shoshone Shopper* newspaper as we passed through the double glass doors into the restaurant. I wheeled the old Cheyenne Indian to a booth by the window where I could keep an eye on the truck and on Dog and where we could hear Montana Slim singing "Roundup in the Fall" through his nose on a radio in the kitchen.

"Nineteen-forty-eight 8N tractor, only twelve hundred dollars." He held his gray and black hair back with a suntanned, wrinkled hand. "Comes with a Dearborn front-end loader."

I tipped my hat back, pulled a menu from the napkin holder, and looked at the tiny rainbows at the corners of his thick glasses. "I don't need a tractor, Lonnie."

"It is a good price. Um hmm, yes, it is so."

I nodded, tossed the menu on the table, and glanced around. "You think there's anybody here?"

He blinked and looked over my shoulder toward the cash register. My gaze followed his — two sets of eyes stared at us, just above the surface of the worn-out, wood-grained Formica counter.

"So, you weren't here when it happened?"

The Big Horn County deputy continued to take my statement; he was young, and I didn't know him. "Nope, we just stopped in for a little dinner and noticed that everybody was hiding."

"And you're headed to Billings?"

I wondered what that had to do with anything. "Yep."

"And the old Indian is with you?"

I had listened as he'd questioned Lonnie Little Bird and hadn't liked his tone. "Lonnie."

He stopped scribbling. "Excuse me?"

I looked at my friend, now parked at the corner booth and still studying the *Shopper.* "His name is Lonnie. Lonnie Little Bird. He's an elder and a member of the Northern Cheyenne Tribal Council."

The deputy gave me a long, tough-guy stare, or as much of one as he'd been able to cultivate in the six weeks he had spent at the Montana Law Enforcement Academy in Helena. He stabbed the still shiny black

23

notepad with his pen for emphasis. "I've got that in my notes."

"Good." He gave me more of the look, so I smiled at him. "Then it won't be hard for you to remember his name."

"You didn't see anybody when you pulled in?"

"Nope."

"No Indian male, approximately twenty-five years of age with a . . ."

"She didn't say Indian. She said 'dark hair with dark eyes.' "

He didn't like being interrupted, and he liked being corrected even less. "Look, Mister . . ."

I made him look at the notebook for my name.

A tall, heavyset man entered the café; he wore a large silver-belly hat, a .357 revolver, and a star. He waved at the two behind the counter as I turned back to the deputy. "Wanda's Crow. If she thought he was Indian, she'd have said so."

I caught the eye of the woman with the hairnet. "Wanda, was the kid Indian?" After a brief conversation with the manager, they both shook their heads no. "You need to quit jerking us around, get a more detailed description of the suspect, and put a unit out to circle the vicinity."

24

"Is that what you'd do?" He studied the notebook again for my name — evidently he wasn't a quick learner.

I watched as the large man with the star stood behind his deputy. Wesley Burrell Best Bayles, the sheriff of Big Horn County, was a legend; hell, I'd seen him eat the MONTANA BREAKFAST! SERVED ALL DAY! AS FEATURED IN READER'S DIGEST!

"Son, don't you recognize the highly decorated peace officer of Absaroka County, Wyoming?"

After telling the deputy to get in his unit and ride surveillance, Wes excused him and drank a cup of coffee while I talked to the manager. Ray Bartlett said a guy had come in and asked for a job, so he had given him an application. The kid had sat in the corner booth till a couple of rodeo cowboys finished up at the buffet and departed. He had worked up his nerve, come up to the register, pulled a .22 pistol from his waistband, stuck it in Wanda Pretty On Top's face, and demanded the cash. Wanda, figuring the $214 wasn't worth her life and unsure if the .22 would kill her or just hurt real bad, handed it over. He asked for the change, and she had sighed and then dutifully dumped the coins into a deposit bag. The kid made them get down on the floor, which

Wanda said was fine with her 'cause she was dying to get off her feet. Then he told them that if they moved in the next ten minutes, he'd shoot 'em. Ray said that it had been about five when we came in.

Wes filled himself another and motioned toward me, but I declined. "Ray, what'd the kid look like?"

"Tall, thin . . . stringy long hair and a straw cowboy hat." Ray thought. "Jeans, a T-shirt, and one of them snap-front western shirts."

I nodded. "Had the tail of the shirt out to cover the gun?"

"Yep."

"Anything else?"

Ray thought some more. "He smelled, and he had bad teeth."

I looked to Wes and watched as he plucked the mic from his shoulder and called in the description to the deputies and assorted HPs he had out prowling. We shook hands.

"Thanks, Walt."

"You bet."

I walked to the booth and knocked on the table to get Lonnie's attention. "You ready to go?"

He nodded enthusiastically but kept reading. "They switched the electrical system over to twelve volts." He looked up. "I don't

26

know why people do that; the six-volt system is a good one. Um hmm, yes, it is so."

I loaded Lonnie, folded up his wheelchair, and let Dog out. I watched as the beast relieved himself and memorized every smell between the lamppost and the truck, then let him in the back and fastened my seat belt. Lonnie was still reading the *Shopper,* and it was beginning to worry me. "You all right?"

He didn't look up but continued reading. "Yes."

I waited a minute. "I apologize for that."

He still didn't look at me. "For what?"

"The deputy in there."

He finally turned his head. "Why should you apologize for him?" I stared through the windshield and started backing out. "Where are we going, Walter?"

I thought Lonnie must have been getting forgetful. "Well, we were going to your doctor's appointment, but it's so late, we'll have to go home and reschedule."

He looked back at the paper. "Oh, I thought you might want to go get the young man who robbed the café."

It was a rundown trailer park on the outskirts of Hardin, the kind that attracted tornados and discarded tires. We cruised the loop and stopped just short of a sun-weathered single-wide with a rusted-out Datsun pickup parked in the grassless yard. A television cast its flickering blue light across the curtained windows, and Wesley Bayles, Ray Bartlett, and I turned to look at Lonnie, who folded his paper and glanced at the number on the dented mailbox alongside the dirt driveway. "This is it, 644 Roundup Lane, Travis Mowry. Um hmm, yes, it is so."

I shrugged, placed my hat on the dash, and reached my arm behind the seat. "Can I borrow your gun?" Wes handed me his sidearm, and, quietly closing the door behind me, I got out of the truck. I stuffed the big Colt in the back of my jeans as Wes got out on the passenger side with an 870 Remington he'd brought from his vehicle.

I glanced over to make sure the interior lights of the truck had gone out. It was fully dark now, and the trailer park gave me an advantage by not having any streetlights.

I pulled out my wallet, rolled all the cash I had into a substantial wad, and then mounted the rickety aluminum stairs to knock on the screen door. I could make out the kitchenette and the carpet strip that led to what I assumed was the living room. Some reality show was playing on the television, and I had to knock again. After a moment, a weedy looking young woman came to the door and looked at me. She did not open the screen and had the look of someone who had taken life on early, made some bad choices, and had gotten her ass kicked.

I grinned and, making sure she could see the twenty on top, gestured with the bills. "Is Travis around?" She looked uncertain. "I've got this money that John gave me to give to him? I know it's late, but I thought he might need it?" It was a calculated risk, but everybody knew a John.

She still didn't come close to the screen, and her voice was thin and halting. "You can give it to me."

Always let them see the money.

I shook my head but continued to smile. "I'm sorry, ma'am, but I don't know you. Is Travis here?"

She didn't say anything but turned and disappeared.

I took a deep breath, glanced back to the truck, and wondered, if there was trouble, what Wes thought he could do from out there.

I heard footsteps and watched as a tall,

lanky young man stopped in the hallway. He wore dirty jeans, boots, and a grimy, wifebeater T-shirt. He was holding a can of Coors Light and smoking a cigarette. "Who're you?"

"I'm a friend of John's. I was supposed to bring this money over to you?"

"John who?"

It appeared not everyone knew a John after all. I took another calculated risk — they were working so well. "John from the bar? I mean you are Travis Mowry, right?" I held up the cash. "Something about some money for you?"

Always let them see the money.

He stepped forward, pushed open the screen door, and reached for the roll of bills. I let him have it but then grabbed his wrist and, slipping the .357 from the back of my jeans and lodging it under his jaw, yanked him from the trailer in one heave. I turned the two of us back toward the truck. The doors were open, Wes was running across the yard with the shotgun, and the manager was nodding his head *yes*.

Ten minutes later, we were booking Travis Mowry at the Big Horn County jail under the watchful eyes of two Montana highway patrolmen and three deputies, including the one who had questioned us at the Blue Cow. It appeared that the majority of eastern Montana law enforcement wanted to know how, after we'd stumbled onto a relatively cold 10-52, we had apprehended the suspect in less than twenty minutes.

Travis had a four-page rap sheet, starting with his stealing a car at the age of fourteen. He got caught and was remanded to juvenile detention. He got out, stole another car, got caught, was sent to a foster home, ran away, and stole yet another until he graduated to producing methamphetamine in a bathtub. He had done a two-spot in Deer Lodge, where the prison psychologist intimated that it was all a question of comparison, but that if you sat a bag of groceries next to Travis, the groceries would get into Stanford before he would.

The police officers stood a little away from Lonnie but snuck glances at him as he continued to read the *Shoshone Shopper* in Big Horn County's basement jail as I finished up my written statement.

Wes tugged at my sleeve. "All right, how did you know?"

I looked at the old Indian, who folded his paper in his lap and waited along with the legendary Wesley Burrell Best Bayles and the collected force for my reply. "Why, Wes, that was just top-flight investigative work." I looked back at the group and tipped my hat, especially at the narrow-minded deputy. "You fellas have a nice night."

I waited. We were racing a 150-car Burlington Northern Santa Fe down the Little Big Horn Valley, another famed site of monumental hubris and stupidity. There was a slight breeze rustling the sage and the buffalo grass, the obelisk and markers of the Seventh Cavalry almost discernible in the light of the just-risen moon. Lonnie remained quiet, his veined arm resting on the doorsill, his thick-lensed glasses reflecting the stripe of the Milky Way stretching from horizon to horizon, what the Indians called the Hanging Road.

"Did I ever tell you about that rattlesnake I ran over with my father's 8N tractor?" I sighed and wondered what sort of pithy homespun philosophy this story would turn out to illustrate. "When I got back from Korea, he had two hay fields, and one was about three miles down the county road. It was a Friday afternoon, and I had just finished cutting. I was a young man, and in a hurry, but I saw this big rattler sunning himself on the road. Not the smartest thing to do." He chuckled. "He was a big one;

had twelve buttons on him —"

"All right, Lonnie, how did you know it was Travis Mowry?" He turned to look at me, hurt at my interrupting his story. "And how the hell did you know that he lived at 644 Roundup Lane?"

He half smiled, and his eyes returned to the stars as he nodded with his words. "OIT."

I thought about the well-known phrase. "Old Indian trick?"

He continued nodding and carefully pulled Travis Mowry's Blue Cow Café employment application from the folds of his newspaper. He handed it to me — the form was completely filled out.

"Um hmm, yes, it is so."

# MINISTERIAL AID

*The Millennium: January 1, 2000 — 6:20 A.M.*
I was driving south on I-25 and kept sneaking glances through my half-closed eyes in hopes of seeing those first, dull, yellow rays of daylight crawling up from the horizon.

My county in northern Wyoming is approximately seven thousand square miles — about the size of Vermont or New Hampshire — and it's a long way from one end to the other, especially in times of crisis, so in my line of work it pays to have a substation.

Powder Junction, the second largest town in Absaroka County, straddles the foothills of the Bighorn Mountains and the Powder River country and is forty-five minutes of straight-as-an-arrow driving from Durant, the county seat. This little settlement of five hundred brave souls is where I subject at least one of the deputies on my staff to some of the most bucolic duty they'll likely ever withstand in a lifetime of law enforcement.

I didn't make it down here very often — in fact, I hadn't made it much of anywhere since my wife, Martha, had died a few months earlier. The reason I was here, very hungover and very early on New Year's Day, was because I owed Turk Connally, the lone member of my Powder Junction staff, a paycheck. I hadn't gotten it to him on Friday, which was payday, because it was New Year's Eve. The reason I was driving the hundred miles round-trip to hand-deliver Turk's check instead of mailing it was that I had gotten into an altercation with the county commissioners over the price of stamps. Since they pay for my gas, I thought I'd teach them a lesson.

As I drove along, with a thrumming headache, I began wondering to whom it was I was teaching that lesson.

Turk generally slept late but especially the morning after a holiday, so I knew he wouldn't be at the office. I unlocked the door of the old Quonset hut that served as our headquarters south and left his check on the desk.

I was on my way out when the rotary-dial phone rang. I knew that after three rings the call would be transferred to the rented house where Turk lived, so in the spirit of the season I decided to cut the kid a break and answer it. "Absaroka County Sheriff's Department."

The voice was female and uncertain. "Turk?"

"Nope, it's Walt."

There was a pause. "Who?"

"Walt Longmire, the sheriff."

"Oh, I'm sorry, Walt. I must've dialed the Durant number . . ."

"No, I'm here in Powder Junction. How can I help you?"

She adjusted the phone, and I could hear another voice in the background as she fumbled with the receiver. "It's Elaine Whelks, the Methodist preacher down here, and I'm over at the Sinclair station by the highway." There was another pause. "Walt, I think we've got a situation."

My head pounding, I drove the short distance through town and under the overpass past the entrance to the rest stop and turned into the service station. I noticed a late-model Buick parked at the outskirts of the lot over near the sign that advertised gas at $1.54 a gallon to passing motorists, a price that would definitely teach the commissioners. It was still mostly dark as I parked between a tan sedan and a Jeep Cherokee, climbed out of my four-year-old Bronco, which was adorned with stars and light bars, and trudged inside.

There were two women holding steaming Styrofoam cups of coffee who were seated on some old café chairs to the left of the register. They both looked up at me as I stood by their table.

"Happy New Year."

They said nothing.

"I'm Walt Longmire."

They still stared at me, but maybe it was my bathrobe.

"The sheriff." I glanced down at the old, off-white, pilled housecoat, a gift from my newly dead wife. "I wasn't planning on making any public appearances today."

The older woman in the purple, down-filled jacket extended her hand. "Elaine Whelks, Sheriff. I'm the one who called." She looked at the robe again and then quickly added, "I knew Martha through the church, and I'm so sorry about your loss. She was a wonderful woman."

I squeezed the bridge of my nose with a thumb and forefinger and gave the automatic response I'd honed over the last couple of months. "Thank you."

The younger woman, heavyset and wearing a Deke Latham Memorial Rodeo sweatshirt, rose and smiled at me a little sadly.

37

"Would you like a cup of coffee, Sheriff?"

I nodded my head and sat on one of the chairs. "Sure."

The older woman studied me, and she looked sad, too; maybe it was just me, but everybody seemed sad these days. She dipped her head to look me in the eyes. "I'm the Methodist minister over at St. Timothy's."

I nodded. "You said."

"How are you doing, Walt?"

The throbbing in my head immediately got worse. "Hunky-dory."

Her eyes stayed on me. "I don't think I've ever seen your hair this long."

I pushed it back from my face, and it felt like even the follicles ached. "I've been meaning to get it cut, but I've been kind of busy."

She changed the subject. "How's Cady?"

I laughed but immediately regretted it.

"Something funny, Sheriff?"

My daughter was in law school in Washington and had been in Crossroads to keep me company over the holidays. I shrugged, thinking that if I could get this over with quick, I could go home and back to sleep, sleeping being a part-time occupation lately. "We had a fight last night."

"You and Cady?"

I nodded. "She got mad; went back to Seattle." Breaking off the conversation, I looked out the window. "Maybe you'd better tell me what it is you need my assistance with."

The preacher sighed and then gestured toward the other woman, who was on her way back to the table with my cup of coffee. "She called me this morning and said that Jason, the young man who works nights, left her a note that a woman was parked at the end of the lot."

Liz set the large cup in front of me along with a bowl of creamers and some sugar packets; I didn't know her, so she didn't know my habits. "Black is fine. Thanks." I took a sip — it was hot and good.

"We generally don't pay very much attention to these types of things. People get tired and pull off the interstate; maybe they feel more comfortable over here with someone around than at the rest stop — a woman especially."

I pulled my hair back again — I was going to have to ask my old friend Henry Standing Bear for a leather strap if I didn't get a haircut pretty soon — and sipped the coffee, dribbling a little on the table. "Uh-huh."

"But she was still here this morning when

I opened up."

I set my cup back down. "I see."

Liz glanced over my shoulder toward the parking lot. "She came over about twenty minutes ago and filled her tank — used the credit card machine and then pulled back there again."

I glanced behind me, eyeing the vehicle. "She ran it all night?"

Elaine nodded her head. "That's the only way you'd be able to stay out there, as cold as it is."

"Local or out-of-state plates?" They both looked at me blankly as I turned my cup in the coffee I'd spilled. "Did you talk to her?"

"I did." Liz pointed at the minister. "And then I called her."

Looking back at Elaine and then over to Liz, I thought about how in some instances my staff and I also contacted the local clergy to provide assistance to needy travelers. "She needed ministerial aid?"

The two women looked at each other, then the pastor turned back to me. "She says she's waiting on the Messiah."

I laughed. "Aren't we all?"

Elaine leaned in close but then retreated a little, probably from the smell. I hadn't been bathing regularly, being so busy sleeping. "I'm serious, Sheriff. She says she's supposed to meet Him. Here. Today."

I wasn't sure if I'd heard her right. "Jesus?"

"Yes."

"Jesus." I sighed, glancing around trying not to cast aspersions, but it was hard. "Returning after two thousand years and He chooses the Sinclair station in Powder Junction, Wyoming?"

"Apparently."

I ran my hand through my beard. "Well, I guess I'd better go talk to her."

As I stood, Elaine held out a roll of breath mints. "Maybe you should have a few of these . . . for the coffee, you know?"

Liz touched the stained sleeve of my bathrobe but only briefly. "And, Sheriff?" She looked out the window. "She has a knife."

There are twenty-four counties in Wyoming, and each one's assigned number sits in front of Steamboat, the bucking horse that is the symbol for the state on the longest-running license plate design in the world. Absaroka, being the least populated, gets twenty-four — the number that was on the Buick — so it was not only in-state but also in-county. Stumbling across the snow-covered parking lot in my moccasins, I approached the car,

41

exhaust clouding the air on the driver's side.

The woman was elderly, probably approaching eighty years of age, dressed in a pair of sweatpants and an oversized parka with fake fur around the collar.

Standing there on the hard-packed snow, I tapped on the window.

It startled her, and I could clearly see the butcher knife clutched in her hands as she turned to look at me. Her face was wet from tears, one of her eyes was swollen shut, and I was betting she had a full-blown headache to match mine. She stared at me the same way the ladies in the convenience store had.

I watched my breath cloud the window between us as the wind lifted the hem of the bathrobe. "Hey, could I speak with you for a moment?"

She sat there with her mouth a little open and then began fumbling at finding the window button, but when she did, it only whined a little and then pulled at the rubber weather seal at the top — frozen shut.

I gestured toward the passenger-side door. "How 'bout I come around and get in?"

She nodded, and I ambled my way around the four-door and pulled on the handle — it too, frozen shut. Unwilling to take no for an answer, I put all six feet five inches and two hundred and thirty pounds behind the effort and almost took the door off. I quickly climbed in and slammed it shut behind me.

It seemed warmer in the car, but not by much. The radio was on some AM station, and a guy was screaming about it being the Millennium, and therefore the end of the world, and about salvation and a bunch of other stuff. I didn't think my head could hurt any more than it already did, but the radio was so loud that the pain escalated. I reached up, turned the thing off, and looked at her. "Sorry, I can't take that crap."

She stared at me with her mouth still hanging open.

I was ready to rest my head on the dash but figured I'd better see what was what first. I stamped the snow off my moccasins onto the rubber floor mats. "Lot of snow."

She nodded.

I gestured toward the weapon in her hands. "Mind if I have the knife?"

Without hesitation, she handed it to me, and I placed it on the floor by my feet. I turned back to look at her, but she was the first to speak. "You . . . You're bigger than I thought you'd be."

It seemed like an odd thing to say, especially since I was pretty sure I didn't know her. "I get that a lot." She seemed to want more, so I added, "From my father's side."

She nodded, studying me. "I understand."

I straightened the collar of my robe. "I apologize for the way I'm dressed, but I really wasn't planning on going out today."

"That's okay."

She started crying, and I felt a little empathetic twinge. "I've had some problems of my own as of late . . ."

She nodded enthusiastically, wiping the tears away with the back of a hand aged with spots and wrinkled skin, careful to avoid the wounded eye. "Me, too."

I held my fingers out to the heater vents, stretching them as a matter of course, buying time till my head stopped hurting enough so that I could concentrate. "I guess that's what this life is all about, getting from one trouble to the next, at least in my job."

She turned in the seat. "I would imagine; and you get everybody's problems."

"Pretty busy, especially during the holidays."

"Yes." Her eyes shone. "Everybody thought I was crazy, but I said you'd come."

I looked around and yawned, the popping in my head sounding like gunshots. "Well, when we get a call . . ." I sat there for a moment longer, looking at her, and then reached a hand out and touched her cheek.

"Tell me about this problem."

She ducked her head away but then reached up and took my hand, holding it in her lap like she had held the knife. She didn't say anything, and we just sat there, listening to the Buick's motor running and the fan of the heater. "He doesn't mean to do it."

"Uh-huh."

"But I forget things." She sobbed a little. "I just don't remember like I used to." She stared at the dash, the instruments glowing a soft green.

It was a modest home on the outskirts of town, a single-level ranch, the kind that can contain a lot of rage. There was a yellowed-plastic, illuminated Santa in the yard, and I was surprised that when we met at the front of the car, she looked at it and then at me and said, "I hope you don't mind."

Wondering what she was talking about, I glanced at the jolly old elf and decided not to judge. "Um, no. I'm a big fan myself."

Her spirits appeared buoyed. "Oh, good."

Oddly, she took my hand again, and we walked up the shoveled walk to the front porch, a gold cast emanating from a needless bug bulb. As we stood there, she threaded her fingers into her parka and produced a prodigious key ring.

Suddenly, the door was yanked open, and a bald man with a Little League baseball bat in one hand was yelling at the two of us through the storm door; another wave of pain ricocheted around in my head.

"Where the hell have you been? Do you know there's no damn cigarettes in this house?" Peering through heavily framed glasses, he glanced up at me. "And who the hell is this?"

Her head, having dropped in embarrassment, rose as she clutched my arm. "This, Ernie, is our Lord and Savior."

I stopped pinching my nose in an attempt to relieve the pain and turned to look down at her. She smiled a hopeful smile, and then we both turned to look at her husband.

He stood there for a moment staring first at her, then at me, and then back to her before leaning the baseball bat against the doorjamb. "Jesus H. Christ."

She smiled and nodded. "That's right."

I smiled — it seemed like the thing to do.

He pushed open the storm door, reached out, grabbed her hand, and half yanked her into the house. "God damn it, get in here before you wander out into traffic."

He tried to close the door, but I caught it and held it open. He struggled, but I figured

I had him by a hundred and fifty pounds. His eyes had a panicked look. "You're not coming in here."

I took the aluminum frame in my other hand and pulled him through onto the porch. "Nope, you're coming out here." I looked in at the elderly woman and smiled reassuringly, holding up my index finger. "We'll be just a minute."

She nodded and gave me a little wave.

I turned to the old man, who had shuttled toward the corner of the porch like a sand crab. He looked uncertain and then spoke in a low voice. "Look, if you're a hobo and need some change . . ."

I shook my head.

He studied my bathrobe, even going so far as to check my wrists for a medical bracelet. "If you're from some loony bin . . ."

I took my hand down and leaned on the other side of the door. "Do you know who I am?"

He clutched his arms in an attempt to ward off the cold. "Well, I know you're not Jesus Christ."

"I'm Walt Longmire, the sheriff of this county."

He adjusted his glasses and leaned in, peering through my beard and hair, finally

47

leaning back and nodding his head. "So you are." On more solid ground, he smirked. "I hear tell you're a drunk."

I looked out in the yard toward the east where the sun was still struggling to shoot a beam over the frozen ground of the Powder River country. "Is that what they say?"

His teeth were starting to chatter now. "Yeah, it is."

I stretched my jaw in a wide yawn again and tried to feel the cold, but it just wasn't there; in all honesty, I just wanted to feel something, anything. Maybe that's why I'd drunk so much after Cady left last night. "Well, they might be right." I straightened my robe. "My wife died a couple of months ago." I threaded my fingers through my beard and felt crumbs in there. "It wasn't a perfect marriage by any means; we fought, about stupid things — when our daughter should go to bed, the color of the mailbox, money . . . But she was the best thing that ever happened to me." I took a deep breath and exhaled, watching the twin clouds of vapor roll across my chest like a cartoon bull. "Maybe the best thing that ever will."

He glanced at the closed door and then at the house slippers on his feet.

I flicked my eyes to the door as well. "She seems nice."

He nodded. "Esther, her name is Esther." He automatically stuck out his hand. "And I'm Ernie — Ernie Decker."

I shook his hand and noticed the swelling and bruises. "Nice to meet you, Mr. Decker."

He quickly tucked the hand back under his arm. "We've hit a rough patch these past few months."

"Well, at least you've got her to have a rough patch with."

We stood there for a while longer, then I pushed off the doorjamb and started toward the steps; I stopped on the second to turn and look at him, my head dropped, hair covering my face, and I was pretty sure that even from this distance, my voice was vibrating his lungs: "You hit her again and I'll be back, and this time it won't take me two thousand years."

I walked down the shoveled path and driveway, took a left on Main, and struck off back the couple of miles toward the highway. After a moment, the tan Oldsmobile that had been parked at the Sinclair station pulled up beside me, and I heard a window whir down.

"Walter?" I stopped and turned to see the Methodist preacher leaning across the seat to look up at me. "I thought I'd follow you and see if you needed a ride back to your truck."

"Thanks." I continued to watch for the sunrise as I tightened the sash on my robe. "But I think I'll just walk."

She paused for a second. "Are you all right?"

"Yep."

"How is the woman in the car?"

Watching the skyline still flat as a burned, black pancake, I chewed on the skin at the inside of my lip. "I think she'll be okay."

"She seemed awfully confused."

Just then, I thought I might've caught sight of that first ray that shoots over the edge of the earth like a hopeful thought, and maybe, just maybe, I might've felt something. "Well, like the rest of us . . ." I sighed. "She's just waiting on something."

# SLICK-TONGUED DEVIL

You steel yourself against those unexpected surprise visits in your mind, but it does nothing to prepare you for the physical evidence of a life shared, a life lost — her voice on the backlogged messages of the answering machine, photographs used as bookmarks, a song she used to hum, people who knew her but didn't really, asking about her in casual conversation. Others telling you they know what it's like when they don't. If you're lucky, you convince yourself that the only real world is the one in your head, and you make a fragile and separate truce that lasts until one of those depth charges erupts and you can no longer run silent or run deep.

It happened at the Busy Bee Café on a Tuesday morning two days before Christmas. As I waited for "the usual," I'd reached across the counter to snag the newly delivered *Durant Courant* and flipped open the first page — and there was my wife's obituary.

I don't know how long I was frozen like that, but when Dorothy, the chief cook and bottle washer of the establishment, refilled my coffee cup, she spotted the grainy black-and-white photograph. I suppose it was her voice, behind me and to the right, that brought me back.

"Oh, Lord."

I went home early from work that day, and nobody asked why.

I parked the Bullet behind the house, because I thought it would be easier to unload the cord of firewood that I'd stored in it through the back door. I draped my uniform shirt and gun belt on the back of my chair and took another shower, put on a flannel shirt, a pair of jeans, and my old moccasins. I opened a can of soup but left it on the counter; then I sat in my chair and drank eleven Rainier beers.

When I looked up, it was sleeting and dark.

The afternoon it happened had been one of those warm November days we sometimes get on the high plains, with a friendly chinook from British Columbia that stays the freeze that can solidify your marrow.

She wanted to sit outside on an old wooden chair I'd bought at the Salvation Army, the red paint peeling away and revealing the gray, weathered wood underneath. "I don't know if that's such a good idea."

Her eyes were closed, but she opened them then, the pale blue matching the Wyoming sky that we could see through the windows of our tiny cabin. "Fresh air is good for you."

I put on the kettle to make tea, wrapped her up in a thick Cheyenne blanket that Henry had given her when she had gotten sick, and carried her outside where she could see the naked trees in the draws of both Piney and Clear Creeks, the branches moving only slightly as if the cottonwoods were stamping their roots to stay warm. "Could you get my Bible?"

I went back in and retrieved her Book from the nightstand downstairs where we'd moved the bed. I placed it carefully in her lap, opened to the marked page. "Here, the feel-good book of the holidays."

I watched as she fit her narrow finger between the pages like a bookmark. She smiled. "You should be more tolerant of things that give people comfort."

I watched a great horned owl drift above

53

one of the creek banks and hitched a thumb into my belt. "Hmm."

"Tough guy." Her fingers climbed up my pant leg and caught my hand there. "You know, a little forgiveness in your character wouldn't hurt."

I glanced down at her. "Not my line of work."

She shook her head at my stubbornness. Except for the mild buffeting of the wind and the chirp of prairie finches, it was silent. "You know, I always thought you'd soften a little with age."

I crouched by her chair, pulled the fine blanket up closer around her shoulders, and ran my hand across her back, the spread of my fingers as large as the trunk of her body. "Hang around. I might surprise you."

She took a slight breath. "I'm trying."

I went back inside at the call of the kettle and returned with two mugs, the paper flags flapping on the ends of the submerged tea bags. It had been a dry fall, and there wasn't enough snow to make it feel like a typical Thanksgiving, and the high desert was warm that afternoon. "It's nice, isn't it?"

She didn't answer.

Being awakened ruined some of the best dreams.

Dog watched as I got up from the La-Z-Boy and tossed the same blanket that Henry had given her over my uniform and gun belt. I walked across the plywood subfloor to the window facing northwest where something was making noise. The wind was picking up, it had started to sleet, and the heavens had gone nickel-plated underneath the darkness.

There were the skeletal poles of a half-erected, Cheyenne-style lodge that the Bear had built in preparation for a New Year's sweat. He hadn't covered it yet, and it hunkered out there in the frozen grass like a naked fan, loose willow branches splayed toward the winter sky.

A few granules of snowy sleet had swept across the ridges along the Bighorn Mountains and collected in the low spots and windward sides of the European blue sage, and on one of the escaped structural limbs of the sweat lodge, a great horned owl sat with his back to me. The Cheyenne believe that owls are messengers of the dead and that they bring word from worlds beyond.

The alcohol was having an effect, like those electronic governors that keep modern cars from going over one hundred and fifty miles an hour, and my thoughts meandered back to the sunny afternoon when my wife had passed and to the days since when the owls had come to impart providence.

I raised an almost-empty Rainier to the window and tapped the aluminum punt against the glass; the large head swiveled and the great golden eyes looked back at me. As the owl watched, I spoke to him with words that clouded the glass.

Dog barked from his spot alongside the sofa and moved over to the unpainted half-panel glass door. I belched, hung an elbow on the sill, and looked at him. When I glanced back, the owl was gone, and the frozen rain was already collecting on the splines of the partially assembled sweat lodge. Dog barked again. I thought I'd heard a knock but, considering the weather, was sure it couldn't be a visitor and that something must've blown against the side of the cabin.

I pushed off the sill and walked past the sofa to the door, placed a hand against the glass, and peered across my porch to the two mud troughs that led across the irrigation ditch to the county road. There was a car parked in the drive close to the house, a taupe-colored Cadillac with Nevada plates. He stood to the side, his back to the wind and rain. The gusts that traveled up the drive blew his long silver hair around his face, and plastered his city-type overcoat against him. He was tall and thin and held some sort of package against his chest.

The man raised his hand to knock again, but when he saw me, he started and froze. I scooted Dog away with my boot and opened the door about ten inches. "Can I help you?"

The man leaned in close and looked at me as he adjusted a pair of wire-rimmed glasses on his long nose. "Do I have the pleasure of addressing Mr. Longmire?" He hunched a shoulder against the wind and ducked his head. "I was wondering if it would be possible for me to speak to Mrs. Longmire?"

In my beer-fogged brain I thought of something Dorothy had said, that these things always happened in threes — the newspaper, the owl, and now this. "I beg your pardon?"

He clutched whatever it was against his chest and pressed himself closer to the doorjamb. "I was wondering if Mrs. Long-mire was available."

I stared at him for only a moment more and then opened the door enough for him to squeeze through. He stood there dripping onto the dirty plywood and then sidestepped, trying to escape Dog's nose in his crotch. Our faces were about eight inches apart — his was thin like the rest of him and, even though he'd been on the stoop for only a short time, his hair was molded to his skull. Underneath the khaki trench coat were an expensive dark suit, a rain-transparent white dress shirt, and a maroon tie the width of a tire tread. One of his hands was clutched around the package, which was in a Tyvek bag.

He pushed Dog's nose away. "Not a fit night for man or beast." He grinned for a moment, and then his features shifted to a look of earnest appeal. "I'm really sorry to be bothering you on a night like this, but is Mrs. Longmire in?"

I stuffed a hand in my jeans and downed the remainder of my beer. He was handsome in a talking-head, newscaster-gone-to-seed sort of way. "What's this about?"

He stood almost at attention, gesturing with the plastic-wrapped package. "Mr. Longmire, my name is Gene Sherman, and I'm from the American Bible Company, and I'm sorry for the delay but the regional office wanted me to make a special trip out here to get this to your wife."

I looked at the dripping bundle. "A Bible?"

He nodded. "Yes, sir."

I crossed the room, crushed the beer can,

and dropped it into the drywall bucket that served as my only trash can. "C'mon in and sit yourself down — dry off." I reached into the fridge that had been sitting on the delivery skids for years and pulled out two cans. "You want a beer?"

He stood by the door, uncertain. "Thank you, but I don't drink, Mr. Longmire, and I've got two more Bibles to deliver before I get to Douglas tonight."

I nodded and gazed at the frozen rain that swooped out of the darkness and crashed against the glass, sliding down and freezing in patterns that looked like bars. "How about a cup of tea?"

He paused but then spoke. "Tea."

I returned one of the cans to the refrigerator, opened mine, took a sip, and stared at him.

"Actually, tea would be nice."

I turned the kettle on with a soft pop of propane, snagged a dishcloth from the handle of the range, and crossed back toward him, handing him the towel. "Here, something to wipe your face off with." I gestured toward the sofa. "Have a seat."

"Thank you." He sat on the edge, his knees together, and reached a hand out to pet Dog, who had returned to his spot beside the couch. "Big dog."

I stood by the back of my recliner, my arms resting on the Cheyenne blanket. "Yes, he is."

"What kind?"

"Heinz, fifty-seven varieties."

He laughed politely, and then there was a long silence, long enough to make him uncomfortable. He glanced down the only hallway in the cabin and up into the loft. "Is Mrs. Longmire in?"

"No, she's not."

He nodded and looked down at the package in his hands. "Are you expecting her?"

"Not particularly."

His eyes came back up. "The reason I ask is that there's a financial remuneration concerning the model she ordered from the American Bible Company. Mrs. Longmire showed exquisite taste in picking the special heritage edition." He carefully shed the Tyvek from the tome and held it out for me to see. There were two other books that still lay swaddled in the bag. It was a very large, leatherlike volume with my wife's name impressed in gilt across the lower right-hand side of the cover.

I took a swig as I marveled at the Bible. "Is that leather?"

He smiled. "Leatherette — superior. It wears better, and that's something to take into consideration with a fine edition such as this that will be gracing your home and your children's homes for years to come."

I stepped back to the particleboard counter, turned over a mug, and retrieved one of the six-year-old tea bags from the cabinet. "I'm afraid all I've got is Earl Grey."

"Oh, that'd be fine." He took a deep breath and looked around, at the unfinished carpentry, the worn furniture, and the general untidiness of the place. "Is she away, visiting family perhaps?"

I crossed from the kitchen to my chair, re-arranged the blanket again, and leaned on the back. "When was it my wife ordered this Bible?"

He did his best to look ashamed. "I'm sorry to say that it was over six weeks ago, which is why the company sent me out personally to deliver the edition." He shrugged. "I'm something of a problem solver — you see, with the special heritage version there are certain artisan aspects that simply can't be rushed. It was a phone order, and I do apologize for any inconvenience that the delay might've caused, but if you'll just have a look at the craftsmanship." He gestured the Bible toward me. "I'm sure that you'll be amazed at the quality of detail."

"How much is it?"

We both listened to the wind pressing the sleet against the log walls of the cabin. "The basic price of this special book is one hundred and forty-two dollars, but with the personalization option — you can see Mrs. Longmire's name in twenty-four-karat gold leaf here on the cover — the total comes to one hundred and eighty-eight dollars, not including tax, which you are exempt from, considering this is an out-of-state purchase."

"And where exactly is the American Bible Company located?"

He showed me his teeth. "Henderson, Nevada — right near Las Vegas. If you're going to produce the Good Book, what better place than Sin City?"

I showed him my teeth in return. "Amen."

He brightened and smiled more broadly. "Are you a religious man, Mr. Longmire?"

I sipped my beer. "Not so much. My wife used to tend to the religion for both of us — my interests were more of this world."

"Used to?"

"My wife is dead, Mr. Sherman."

He rested the Bible on his knee, the other two still lying at his feet, and leaned back as if he'd been struck. "I'm terribly sorry." The wind, snow, and sleet continued to buffet the cabin as we sat there. "Was it sudden?"

"Evidently."

"I'm shocked."

I nodded. "Imagine how I feel."

He shook his head. "I'm terribly sorry for your loss and even sorrier to intrude on your grief."

"Thank you for your concern." The kettle was beginning to grouse.

He nodded enthusiastically but then slowed with dramatic sorrow and held the Bible at an angle where I could easily read my late wife's name. "Your wife, Martha, she was very keen on the idea. I was fortunate enough to speak with her personally."

The kettle roused itself to full voice behind me. "Really?" It was now screaming. "I'd be interested to hear what she had to say — considering she's been dead for six years."

He didn't move.

I took the last sip of my beer, crushed the can, and dropped it into the drywall bucket to join the others. I studied him for a moment more and then stepped to the range, picked up the kettle, and poured hot water into the mug. I stirred the mixture with a spoon and glanced back at him. "Do you take anything in it?"

He still didn't move.

"Do you take anything in your tea?" I

tapped the spoon on the rim of the mug and then carefully placed it on the edge of the sink. "Just as well, because I don't have anything anyway." I purposefully walked over to him and handed him the cup. "Yep, a little mix-up at the local paper."

He swallowed visibly.

I took the Bible from his hand, crossed the room, and plucked the blanket from my recliner, revealing the large-frame Colt .45 in the Sam Browne, and the six-pointed star of the Absaroka County Sheriff attached to my jacket. "Sheriff." I glanced at the star and then at my sidearm. "Sheriff Longmire."

I tossed the blanket onto the chair and sat with my elbows on my knees and the book in my lap. "It was a mistake. Ernie 'Man About Town' Brown went into Durant Memorial for surgery on his prostate and left a manila folder on his desk. His part-timer saw the file folder marked obituaries and assumed they were current."

He still didn't move.

"I'd imagine it's hard to throw away the photos and obituaries of people you know well. Michael Lenz, a friend of Ernie's who had died in a car crash back in the nineties, was there, along with Ernie's sister Yvonne, who passed almost twelve years ago — and my wife, Martha." I stared at the book in my lap. "Those two other Bibles at your feet wouldn't have Michael's and Yvonne's names on them, would they?"

He cleared his throat and spoke. "Mr. Longmire —"

"Sheriff." Another moment passed. "You know, there was this scam that they started to pull in the dirty thirties when cheap presses made mass-market printing possible. These con men would drive around with the trunks of their cars filled with Bibles and they'd pick up the local newspaper and get the names from the obituaries, then they'd print the names on the Bibles and sell them to the aggrieved survivors."

He started to get up slowly, so as to not spill his tea.

I looked at him, my voice a little more than conversational. "Sit down, Mr. Sherman." He stayed there for a second and then eased himself back onto the sofa. Dog, hearing the tone of my voice, planted his big paws on the floor and raised his head to look up at him.

I opened the cover and looked at the cheap, gold-edged pages with color separation that looked like newspaper comics; the inside cover was printed with a large tree with blank lines for family members. It wasn't a very good version of the Good Book, or of any other book for that matter.

"My mother used to drag me to church when I was a kid, and I would sit there looking at the stained glass windows and listening to the choir sing and wondering what the heck was wrong with me." I sighed and flipped a few more of the thin pages. "Never went back."

He cleared his throat, and I glanced at him, but he didn't say anything.

I looked at the Bible in my hands. "What do you suppose is the most important lesson in this Book? That's what it is, right? A book of lessons on how it is we're supposed to treat each other." I took a deep breath. "I mean, if I was to read this, what do you suppose is the most important thing I'd take away from it?"

He looked around, at anything except me. "I'm not sure."

"I think this Book is about forgiveness and tolerance." I looked up at him. "At least, you better hope so." I watched his eyes widen as my hand reached past my duty belt, and I pulled my checkbook from the seat of my jeans and my pen from my jacket pocket, which was just below the star. "One hundred and eighty-eight dollars, right?"

66

We sat there, and I made him look at me.

My eyes stayed steady with his. "Should I make this out to the American Bible Company or to you, Mr. Sherman?" He didn't say anything but just sat there, holding his mug. ". . . I'll just make it out to you." After signing the check and tearing it out, I tucked the Bible under my arm. "Well, it doesn't look as if you enjoy my tea or my company, and I don't want to hold you here any longer."

We stood. I took the mug and handed him the slip of paper.

He held the check.

"Don't worry, it's good, Mr. Sherman — and I'll be happy to deliver those other two Bibles to save you the trouble."

I watched as he turned the expensive car around; he hit the gas, it slid a little, and my eyes followed the taillights as they disappeared down the ranch road.

I walked over to the northwest window where I'd begun the evening and sipped Mr. Sherman's untouched tea; it was still warm. Dog watched me as I pulled the special heritage edition Bible from under my arm and peered through the ice-rimed window to see if the owl had returned.

He hadn't.

Martha and I had argued earlier that afternoon. I don't even remember what it was we'd argued about, but I remember the tone of her voice, the timbre and cadence. It's important to me sometimes to try and remember what it was that had been said, but I can't. I'm afraid that my mind works like that more and more these days, allowing the words spoken to disappear into cracks and crevices.

I thumbed the Good Book open, flipped through a few pages, and then closed it. The sleet had turned to snow, and the flakes caught the light from inside the cabin and burst into small sparks before pressing themselves against the glass.

I continued to look out into the raw night, but from habit my eyes drifted upward and I thought about how maybe I had softened a little, and the words escaped with the memories. "You should've hung around."

# FIRE BIRD

Motivated by a sense of generational snobbery or the assumption that the drink, cuisine, and ambient atmosphere might be better in such places, the ignorant or unwary visitor to Absaroka County, faced with where to revel away the debut of the New Year, might choose the Euskadi Bar, the Centennial, or even Henry's establishment, the Red Pony, over the Durant Home for Assisted Living.

They would, of course, be dead wrong.

The aged of Absaroka County look after their creature comforts with an expertise born of making it through one depression and the war to end all wars. No matter where you are in the county and no matter who goes short, it won't be them — they've been in the game far too long for that.

Ex-mayor Bud "Buddy" Elkins stood next to the Dutch doors of the home's entryway broom closet. Handing me a Pappy Van

Winkle's bourbon, he looked past my shoulder to where the one-legged ex-sheriff was contemplating the latest of my opening chess gambits, Dog at his foot. "Looks like you've got Lucian flummoxed."

There had been times in the last quarter of a century when my old boss and mentor, Lucian Connally, had let me off the hook on chess night, especially on holidays, but tonight was not one of those nights. Evidently, the old sheriff had left a space heater too close to the curtains in room 32 and was being forced to spend New Year's Eve in the communal area, a place he normally avoided like a hot and cold running venereal disease. They had cleaned out his room, but they wouldn't let him return to his haunt until near midnight when they figured the fumes would have dissipated.

I was here as a buffer.

I sipped my drink and glanced back. "He's distracted; he doesn't care for the music and hubbub." I was referring to the pickup Dixieland jazz trio that was playing next to the Christmas tree, which seemed perilously near the roiling flames in the blond-brick fireplace. "That and I picked up a few moves from one of my deputies."

"The Pyrenees Indian?"

I smiled at the old politician's political

incorrectness. "Saizarbitoria — he's the one who's caught the duty tonight."

He sipped his Coke. "What about that hellcat, that other deputy of yours?"

"Vic? She's back in Philadelphia till the day after tomorrow."

"I always like it when you bring her along."

I nodded. "So does Lucian. He likes her breasts."

His ninety-two-year-old face took on a dreamy look, and he held a hand out to palm a not so imaginary body part. "They're nice boobies, just the size of a red wine glass — not too big, not too small."

Pretty much everything Buddy had to say had to do with alcohol or women. He'd owned a number of drinking establishments as far back as I could remember — dance clubs, bars, and package stores. In fact, he'd sold me my first beer. Whether I was of legal age was something neither of us ever brought up.

I leaned against the counter that separated the entryway from the main room and glanced around, meeting the eyes of a woman who, apparently, was the reason Buddy was forced to serve the liquor from outside the official party room. Genevieve McNeil was an incredibly old, bright-eyed

71

Presbyterian with a penchant for elaborate hats. Hard, of few words, she kept a sharp eye on the Old Testament God to make sure *He* didn't get up to any shenanigans she might disapprove of, like granting salvation to Catholics or allowing sheriffs to drink in public.

I nodded to her, but she didn't return my greeting and instead turned away and whispered in the ear of one of her compatriots.

In protest, I took another sip of my bourbon. As I looked around, I remembered that this was the room with the black-and-white photos of the area on the walls. The nearest was of the Fort McKinney parade grounds, where in 1878 an opportunistic commander had filed a claim on the ground underneath the fledgling town to the east under the Desert Land Act.

Major Verling Durant had died unrepentantly a few years later, and his wife was given the deed to the unnamed town. Two hundred and fifty land sales were made that next year, including the one for the courthouse and the future Carnegie Library that had become my office and jail. Juliet Durant was suddenly a very rich woman, and the town at the foot of the Bighorn Mountains had a name.

Buddy noticed me studying the photograph. "Whole town started with larceny and hasn't gotten any better since."

"You'd be in a position to know." Bud had served an unprecedented half-dozen terms as mayor of Durant. I motioned toward the framed photos. "Are some of these new?"

He glanced around the room where it seemed to me a lot of additions had been made. "They're from that trove of photos your buddy Henry found up on the Rez. I guess that old Mennonite preacher took photos of white people, too."

I cleared my throat and gestured my tumbler toward the bottle. "You wanna pour one of those for Lucian, I'll take it over to him."

"Might as well — he paid for the stuff."

I took the two glasses to the communal long table and sat a tumbler at the old sheriff's elbow, on the left where he liked it.

"Well, thank Christ for that and the fact that they don't have those damn Christmas carols playing." He took a nip and cast a glittering gimlet of a dark eye toward the trio. "Do me a favor?"

"What's that?"

"Shoot me."

I smiled. "No."

"It's all I want for the holidays, a bullet in

73

the back of my head." He studied the board and massaged the stump where his leg used to be. "Lousy thirty-seven-cent cartridge . . ."

"Lucian." The Dixieland trio had coaxed a few couples out onto the open area at the end of the table near the Christmas tree. It appeared as if everyone was having a good time — all but one. "If you don't like the communal area, then you shouldn't have set fire to your room."

"I didn't set fire to my damned room." He took another sip to combat the general festive spirit. "Jesus H. Christ — didn't even have that damn thing plugged in. They bring us those fire hazards on that windy side of the building, but they already keep the place so hot you can barely breathe." His eyes came back to mine. "You ever see me plug in that space heater?"

It was true, I hadn't. "Maybe one of the attendants did it."

"Those minimum-wage morons couldn't stick a plug up their ass with both hands."

He grew quiet, and I grew worried. His eyes were on the chessboard, but I knew that wasn't what he was seeing. "Lucian."

Even his voice was distracted. "What?"

"Are you all right?" He didn't answer at first, and I took advantage of the situation to give him a good going-over. His hair was like wire and still the silver it had been for decades, cut in the same manner it had been since he had flown a B-25 Mitchell off the deck of the USS *Hornet* all those years ago. The hard times had not diminished him but had worn him like a good piece of leather. His dark eyes were still bright as searchlights, and the wrinkles around them were like fissures in granite. Maybe it was a reminder of my own mortality, but I hated to think of him as old.

He set the searchlights on me, and his words were heavy and low-pitched. "I think I'm slippin' a little." I stared at him. "I swear I don't remember plugging that thing in or turning it on."

I didn't know what to say, so I said nothing and looked around the room just to make sure my eyes wouldn't water. To my surprise, Genevieve McNeil was motioning to me. I excused myself from my old boss and slid down the bench a few seats, careful to remove my hat. "Mrs. McNeil, Mrs. Percy, how are you ladies?"

Genevieve cast a cold and forbidding eye on me, her feathered cloche balanced on her narrow head, the veil patchworking her gray hair. "Should you be drinking on duty, Sheriff?"

I sat my tumbler on the table. "I'm not on duty, Mrs. McNeil."

The feather on her hat wobbled along with her head, but her eyes stayed steady. It was easy to see that she had been an exuberant daughter of the Women's Christian Temperance Movement. "And what if you are called to duty, Mr. Longmire?"

"I won't be." I smiled at her, but she didn't smile back. "We're perfectly safe, Mrs. McNeil."

"You'd be a pretty judge of that with that friend of yours setting fire to the place only last night." She huffed a breath and glanced at Elaine Percy, sitting next to her, who smiled at me and shrugged.

My attention went back to Genevieve. "I think he only singed the curtains in his room."

She shared another glance with Mrs. Percy. "Drinking, no doubt. You realize he's the only resident with liquor in his room?"

Officially chastised, I placed my hat back on my head and stood. "You ladies have a Happy New Year." I edged my way back toward the chessboard with my bourbon. I was sure that if I had left it on the table, Mrs. McNeil would have quickly watered the plants with it.

Bud Elkins, enjoying a break from his bartending duties and taking advantage of my indecision, threw a hand up to call my attention to another photo on the wall beside the entryway.

I joined him, as I could see that Lucian hadn't moved and was still pondering the small wooden pieces along with his own faculties. Elkins raised a narrow forefinger and pointed at a picture of a sprawling, low-slung building. I shifted and looked at it. "Where's that?"

The ex-mayor shifted with me and smiled. "That was my first dance hall, north of town." He sighed deeply. "Burned down and never got open. Long before your time — back in the dirty thirties."

"After Prohibition?"

He nodded his head, aware that he was talking to the law, even if it was the law with a bourbon in his hand. "You bet."

"What happened?"

"Oh, Bill Miller — before you were born — worked for me and slept in the building since they were just getting ready to lay the hardwood dance floor the next morning. Hell of a carpenter, but the man drank — built the Peters Dance Hall, Hotel Ladore, and the American Legion, too. Anyway, Bill said he'd gotten up to go take a whiz and then had gone back to sleep — man slept like a log — woke up an hour later 'cause he said angels were talkin' to him, and the whole place was on fire. It was an honest-to-God miracle he didn't get burned up alive. It was so late and took so long for the fire department to get out there . . ." His voice trailed off. "Ninety thousand shingles, seventy thousand feet of lumber, twenty thousand dollars. That was a lot of money back then."

"That's a lot of money now." I thought about it. "I think I'm starting to remember the story . . . Didn't they arrest a fellow?"

"George Miller, Bill's brother. They found the oilcan that smelled like kerosene that Otto Hanck, the Mennonite tinsmith from over on Klondike, had made for him. Even had his initials on it — GM. Otto never would say the name of the man who bought the can, but since Miller had a competing dance hall over in Story and was the brother of my handyman, it was pretty much an open and shut case."

"Yep, but didn't the dance hall over in Story burn down the next week?"

There was a shadow of discomfort that played across the old man's eyes. "That it did. There's a photograph of that right over there."

We readjusted ourselves and looked at

another picture. "Hmm."

Buddy pointed to another photo. "And there was one that burned up in Big Horn the week after that."

I swallowed a little more Pappy's to prod my memory. "I'm trying to remember about George Miller . . ."

Bud provided the answer. "Moved away after he got out of Rawlins. Idaho, I think."

"What about the brother, Bill?"

"Drank himself to death."

I moved on to the next photograph, but my mind stayed snagged on the one I'd left behind. "Do you think Bill was an accomplice?"

"Nah, he didn't have the nerve for that kind of thing. He was quite a bit older than his brother, fought in the Great War, although I don't know what was so great about it. He got mustard-gassed, and I don't think he ever got over it." The ex-mayor raised his hand and shook it as if palsied. "Had the shakes, bad. People used to joke that the reason he was such a good carpenter was because he was a natural at sanding."

I nodded and looked at the next photo down the line and what looked like a celebration of some kind, a fishing derby, maybe, with a few individuals that I recognized this time. "Robert Taylor."

"The actor, sure. You remember him being around here, don't you?"

I laughed to myself. He was young in the photograph, and the matinee smile was there, the one that had gotten him the record twenty-four-year contract at MGM. "I remember when he used to come down off the mountain in that Cadillac of his with the steer horns and terrorize every stationary object in town. I actually met him one weekend when I was still in school."

Bud leaned in closer and raised his glasses again, and I started wondering why he wore the things. "Yep, that one was taken when they opened the lodge on the peninsula out at Lake DeSmet." He dropped the glasses and leaned in even further. "Well, speak of the devil." He turned to me and pointed at the photo to a rail-thin man in the back row. "Bill Miller." He laughed and shook his bald head. "No surprise; he must've helped to build that place, too. Hell of a carpenter. You know, now that I think of it, that place partially burnt down, too."

I left my gaze on the doomed man but couldn't help but notice the pretty girl in the hat beside him. With his eye to the gentler sex, Buddy knew where mine had come to rest. He grinned. "I bet you can't guess who that gal is."

I studied the photo — the woman did look vaguely and freshly familiar. "I'm not . . ."

"Genevieve McNeil."

I could feel my eyes widen as I stared at the photo. Something struck me, and I moved back to the photograph of the burned dance hall and the small crowd out front, then I moved and studied the photo before that one and the photo before that.

I looked back over my shoulder past Lucian and the chessboard to where Mrs. McNeil sat with her flock of cronies. After a second, she glanced up to see me looking at her. I swiveled my head to reexamine the third photo and then turned to look at her again, and she wore an expression that I had grown accustomed to seeing in the business of enforcing the law.

I turned back to the ex-mayor. "Genevieve McNeil was married to Bill Miller?"

Distracted by the few residents lining up at the broom closet for holiday cheer, he responded absentmindedly. "About ten years. She finally left him and married a man named McNeil, and it wasn't too long after that that Bill died."

I glanced back again, but Genevieve had returned to conversing with her friends and was now ignoring me. I noticed Lucian waving to get my attention and apologized to Bud for taking him away from his duties as bartender. He laughed, thumped my back with the flat of his bony hand, and returned to the makeshift bar as I ambled back to the chessboard.

"You gonna play chess or gallivant all night?"

I sat and reached down to pet Dog, who was snoring. I played at examining the board and threw out a question. "Hey, Lucian, do you remember when the Antelope Bar on Main Street burned down back in the late seventies?"

He snorted. "When that dumbass in the slurry bomber missed the whole damn thing? Christ, I coulda' hit that building from five thousand feet with a sack of potatoes. Yeah, I remember. Why?"

"Do you recall who the primary witness was?"

Annoyed, he looked up from the board. "The fire?"

"Yep."

He grunted a dismissal. "No."

"Wasn't it Genevieve McNeil?"

He thought about it with his lips pressed together and his heavy eyebrows crouched over his dark eyes. "Mighta' been the old she-buzzard, hell, I don't know — but then, it seems I don't know much lately."

That match and the next one were mine, but then he got focused and beat me three in a row.

It was approaching midnight, and Lucian understood my preference for being home in my cabin on New Year's Eve in case Cady decided to call from Philadelphia. Dog joined me in standing as I picked up my coat. I glanced around the room, but Genevieve had disappeared. "You want me to walk you to your room? I know you don't want to be in here at midnight."

He looked up, half startled. "What, you gonna give me a kiss — or are you afraid I can't find it? Besides, they got it locked."

I pulled out my pocket watch to check and make sure I had plenty of time to get home. "C'mon." Dog followed us as we made our way down the hallway toward room 32, and I looked over my shoulder to make sure that none of the staff was following. Giving his only leg a rest and pulling his briarwood pipe and beaded tobacco pouch from the pocket of his wool vest, the old sheriff leaned against the wall and watched me.

I pulled a credit card from my wallet and slipped it between the facing and the door, about where the catch mechanism was, but it only went halfway.

Lucian cleared his throat and lit his pipe. "They turned 'em so you can't do that anymore."

"Hmm . . ." I put the card back in my wallet. "I guess we have to go back to the old standby." I gripped the knob in both hands, placed a shoulder against the jamb in order to force it away from the catch, and pushed. There was a slight cracking noise, and the door came open. I reached around, unlocked it, and held my arm out to motion Lucian inside.

He glanced at the lock plate and the small area of splintered wood. "You messed up my damn door, not that I ever lock the thing anyway."

I stood in there with Dog; the room smelled a little like burnt chemicals, probably from the flame retardant in the curtains that had caught fire. I looked around and noticed that they hadn't given him the option of another space heater. "You don't ever lock your door?"

"No; why the hell would I do that in here?"

I thought about it. "Well, I'm going to head out." He stood in the middle of the room. "You all right?"

He glanced up and then his eyes went

back to where I assumed the space heater had been. "Yep."

I stood there for a bit, then gave up the ghost and pulled the knob. I was about to walk away when I noticed the door across the hallway open about two inches; when I stopped, it quickly closed.

I weighed my options for a while, banking my hunches, then stepped across the carpeted floor and gently knocked.

The door immediately opened about six inches. "Not ringing in, Mrs. McNeil?"

Her face stiffened, and she took a moment to respond. "I've done a few more of them than you, Mr. Longmire."

"Mrs. McNeil?"

"Yes?"

I glanced down at Dog as he sat on my foot. "I need you to do me a favor."

"And what would that be?"

I looked at her. "No more fires."

She stood there with her mouth opened, and now I was sure; I had nothing, but I was sure. She flinched and, with a fluttering movement, began closing the door, but I caught it in one hand and held it open. "You burned down Elkins's Dance Hall before it could open. There's no way the tinsmith Otto Hanck would've gone to the trouble of painting a man's initials on an oilcan, but he would've for a woman. I knew the Hanck family and they were very religious, but Otto wasn't specifically lying when he told authorities that he'd never tell them the name of the *man* who bought the oilcan. Your ex-husband Bill Miller was noted to be a heavy sleeper, but you woke him before the fire you set got out of hand."

She didn't move, but her eyes dropped to look at Dog.

"I figure you set the chain of events in motion that burned down all those dance halls, pitting the owners against each other — or you did it yourself. Then you set fire to the DeSmet Lodge, but that one didn't go all the way. Is that when Bill found out?"

She didn't answer but continued looking at Dog, who wagged in response.

"That's when you left him, right?" I let out with a deep sigh and was sure she could smell the bourbon on my breath. "Then there was the Antelope Bar on Main Street where you were the primary witness along with a few others for cover. I could go on, but all I've got to go on is hearsay, half-century-old evidence, and you in your hats in the photographs of every burned-down drinking establishment in the county for the last seventy years." I paused and let the weight of my next words take hold. "But the incident that concerns me is the one in room 32 across the hall here." I leaned down with my face very close to hers and could smell the old feathers of her hat and maybe even a little smoke — but maybe that was my imagination. "I don't know when you went into Lucian's room and plugged in that space heater and draped the curtain over it, but I bet I can find out."

Her baleful, beady eyes came up and met mine.

"Don't test me on this, Genevieve. If you do, I'll send you down to Lusk to the women's prison for whatever's left of your miserable life."

I lowered my hand and stood there, not feeling so good about bullying a ninety-year-old woman. I probably didn't need that last part, but I wanted her scared enough to not try it again. She lowered her eyes and closed the door, and I looked at the painted surface. I could hear nothing but I was sure she was still standing on the other side, although the rules had changed now that she knew she was being watched.

After a moment, I turned to find Lucian standing in his own open doorway. "What the hell's going on out here?"

I smiled at the old sheriff. "Nothing." I stepped over to him and put my hand on his shoulder. "Just so you know — you're not losing your faculties."

He looked puzzled for a moment, and then the dark eyes sharpened. "And what makes you so sure of that?"

I glanced behind me at the room across the hall and then back to him, knowing full well he'd figure it out. "A little bird told me."

# UNBALANCED

She was waiting on the bench outside the Conoco service station/museum/post office in Garryowen, Montana, and the only parts of her clothing that were showing beneath the heavy blanket she'd wrapped around herself were black combat boots cuffed with a pair of mismatched green socks. When I first saw her, it was close to eleven at night, and if you'd tapped the frozen Mail Pouch thermometer above her head, it would've told you that it was twelve degrees below zero.

The Little Big Horn country is a beautiful swale echoing the shape of the Bighorn Mountains and the rolling hills of the Mission Buttes, a place of change that defies definition. Just when you think you know it, it teaches you a lesson — just ask George Armstrong Custer and the Seventh Cavalry.

I was making the airport run to pick up Cady, who had missed her connection from

Philadelphia in Denver and was now scheduled to come into Billings just before midnight. The Greatest Legal Mind of Our Time had been extraordinarily upset but calmed down when I'd told her we'd stay in town that night and do some Christmas shopping the next day before heading back home. I hadn't told her we were staying at the Dude Rancher Lodge. A pet-friendly motor hotel that was assembled back in '49 out of salvaged bricks from the old St. Vincent's Hospital, the Dude Rancher was a Longmire family tradition. I loved the cozy feeling of the weeping mortar courtyard, the kitschy ranch-brand carpets, and the delicious home-cooked meals in the Stirrup Coffee Shop.

Cady, my hi-tech, sophisticated, urban-dwelling daughter, hated the place.

In my rush to head north, I hadn't gassed up in Wyoming — luckily, the Conoco had after-hours credit card pumps. As I was putting gas into my truck with the motor running, I noticed her stand up and trail out to where I stood, the old packing blanket billowing out from around her shoulders.

Looking at the stars on the doors and then at me, she paused at the other side of the truck bed, her eyes ticktocking. She studied my hat, snap-button shirt, the shiny brass name tag, and the other trappings of authority just visible under my sheepskin coat.

I buttoned it the rest of the way up and looked at her, expecting Crow, maybe Northern Cheyenne, but from the limited view afforded by the condensation of her breath and the cowl-like hood of the blanket, I could see that her skin was pale and her hair dark but not black, surrounding a wide face and full lips that snared and released between the nervous teeth.

"Hey." She cleared her throat and shifted something in her hands, still keeping the majority of her body wrapped. "I thought you were supposed to shut the engine off before you do that." She glanced at the writing on the side of my truck. "Where's Absaroka County?"

I clicked the small keeper on the pump handle, pulled my glove back on, and rested my elbow on the top of the bed as the tank filled. "Wyoming."

"Oh." She nodded but didn't say anything more.

About five nine, she was tall, and her eyes moved rapidly, taking in the vehicle and then me; she had the look of someone whose only interaction with the police was being rousted — she feigned indifference with a touch of defiance and maybe was just a little crazy. "Cold, huh?"

I was beginning to wonder how long it was going to take her and thought about how much nerve she'd had to work up to approach my truck; I must've been the only vehicle that had stopped there in hours. I waited. The two-way radio blared an indiscernible call inside the cab, the pump turned off, and I removed the nozzle, returning it to the plastic cradle. I hit the button to request a receipt, because I didn't trust gas pumps any more than I trusted those robot amputees over in Deadwood.

I found the words the way I always did in the presence of women. "I've got a heater in this truck."

She snarled a quick laugh, strained and high. "I figured."

I stood there for a moment more and then started for the cab — now she was going to have to ask. As I pulled the door handle, she started to reach out a hand from the folds of the blanket but then let it drop. I paused for a second more and then slid in and shut the door behind me, snapped on my seat belt, and pulled the three-quarter-ton down into gear.

She backed away and retreated to the bench as I wheeled around the pumps and stopped at the road. I sat there for a moment, where I looked at myself and my partner in the rearview mirror, then shook my head, turned around, and circled back in front of her. She looked up again as I rolled the window down on the passenger-side door and raised my voice to be heard above the engine. "Do you want a ride?"

Balancing her needs with her pride, she sat there. "Maybe."

I sighed to let her know that my Good Samaritan deeds for the season weren't endless and spoke through the exhaust the wind carried back past the truck window. "I was offering you a lift if you're headed north."

She looked up at the empty highway and was probably thinking about whether she could trust me or not.

"I have to be in Billings in a little over an hour to pick up my daughter." It's always a good idea to mention other women in your life when faced with a woman in need. "Are you coming?"

The glint of temper was there again, but she converted it into standing and yanked something up from her feet — a guitar case that I hadn't noticed before. She indifferently tossed it into the bed of my truck, still carefully holding the blanket around her with the other hand, her posture slightly off.

"You want to put your guitar in here, there's room."

She swung the door open, gathered the folds up around her knees, and slid in. "Nah, it's a piece of shit." She closed the door with her left hand and looked at the metal clipboard, my thermos, and the shotgun locked to the transmission hump. She blinked, and her eyes half closed as the waft of heat from the vents surrounded her, and we sat there longer than normal people would have. After a while her voice rose from her throat: "So, are we going or what?"

"Seat belt." She opened her eyes and looked out the passenger window, and I placed her age at early twenties.

"Don't believe in 'em." She wiped her nose on the blanket, again using her left hand.

We didn't move, and the two-way crackled as a highway patrolman took a bathroom break. She looked at the radio below the dash and then back at me, pulled the shoulder belt from the retractor, and swiveled to put it in the retainer at the center just as my partner swung his furry head around from the backseat to get a closer look.

"Shit!" She jumped back against the door, and something slid from her grip and fell onto the rubber floor mat with a heavy thump.

I glanced down and could see it was a small, wood-gripped revolver.

She slid one of her boots in front of it to block my view, and we stared at each other for a few seconds, both of us deciding how it was we were going to play it.

"What the hell, man . . ." She adjusted the blanket, careful to completely cover the pistol on the floorboard.

Thinking about what I was going to do, I sat there without moving for a moment, then pulled onto the frontage road, and headed north toward the on-ramp of I-90. "That's my partner — don't worry, he's friendly."

She stared at the hundred-and-fifty-plus pounds of German shepherd, Saint Bernard, and who knew what. She didn't look particularly convinced. "I don't like dogs."

"That's too bad — it's his truck."

I eased the V10 up to sixty on the snow-covered road and motioned toward the battered thermos leaning against the console. "There's coffee in there."

She looked, first checking to make sure the gun was hidden, and then reached down, and paused long enough so that I noticed her bare hands, strong and deft even with the remains of the cold. There was something else, though — a plastic medical bracelet, the kind you get at the hospital to remind them who you are.

She saw me watching her and quickly pulled the sleeve of her stained sweatshirt down to cover the municipal jewelry. Then she lifted the thermos by the copper-piping handle, connected to the Stanley with two massive hose clamps, and read the sticker on the side: DRINKING FUEL. She twisted off the top and filled the chrome cap. "You got anything to put in this?"

"Nope."

She rolled her eyes and crouched against the door like a cornered badger. "Good coffee."

"Thanks." I threw her a tenuous, conversational line and caught a glimpse of a nose stud and what might've been a tattoo at the side of her neck. "My daughter sends it to me."

The two-way squawked again as the highway patrolman came back on duty, and she glared at it. "Do we have to listen to that shit?"

I smiled and flipped the radio off. "Sorry, force of habit."

She glanced back at Dog, who regarded her indifferently as she nudged one foot toward the other in an attempt to push the revolver up onto her other shoe. "So, you're a sheriff in Wyoming?"

"Yep."

She nonchalantly reached down, feigning an itch in order to snag the pistol. She slid it back under the blanket and carried it onto her lap. "Your daughter live in Billings?"

"Philadelphia."

She nodded and murmured something I didn't catch.

"Excuse me?"

Her eyes came up, and I noticed they were an unsettling shade of green. "Philly Soul. The O'Jays, Patti LaBelle, the Stylistics, Archie Bell & the Drells, the Intruders . . ."

"That music's a little before your time, isn't it?"

She sipped her coffee and turned to stare out the windshield. "Music's for everybody, all the time."

We drove through the night. It seemed as if she wanted something, and I made the mistake of thinking it was talk. "The guitar case — you play?"

She watched the snow that had just started darting through my headlights again. "Your dog sure has a nice truck." We drifted under the overpass at the Blue Cow Café and Casino as an eighteen-wheeler, pushing the speed limit, became more circumspect in his velocity when I pulled from the haze of snow behind him and passed.

There was another long pause, and the muffled sound of the tires gave the illusion that we were riding on clouds. "I play guitar — lousy. Hey, do you mind if we power up the radio? Music, I mean."

I stared at her for a moment and then gestured toward the dash. She fiddled with the SEEK button on FM, but we were in the dead zone between Hardin and Billings.

"Not much reception this close to the Rez; why don't you try AM — the signals bounce off the atmosphere and you can get stuff from all over the world."

She flipped the radio off and slumped back against the door. "I don't do AM." She remained restless, glancing up at the visors and at the console. "You don't have any CDs?"

I thought about it and remembered that Henry had bought some cheap music at the Flying J truck stop months ago on a fishing trip to Fort Smith, Montana. The Cheyenne Nation had become annoyed with me when I'd left the radio on SEARCH for five minutes, completely unaware that it was only playing music in seven-second intervals. "You know, there might be one in the side pocket of that door."

She moved and rustled her free hand in the holdall, finally pulling out a $2.99 *The Very Best of Merle Haggard.* "Oh, yeah."

She plucked the disc from the cheap cardboard sleeve and slipped it into a slot in the dash I'd never used. The lights of the stereo came on and the opening lines of Haggard's opus "Okie From Muskogee" thumped through the speakers. She made a face, looked at the cover, and read the fine print. "What'd they do, record it on an eight-track through a steel drum full of bourbon?"

"I'm not so sure they sell the highest fidelity music in the clearance bin at the Flying J."

Her face was animated in a positive way for the first time as the long fingers danced off the buttons of my truck stereo, and I noticed the blue metal-flake nail polish and the bracelet that clearly read LAKESIDE PSYCHIATRIC HOSPITAL — LAKESIDE, TN.

"You've got too much bass, and the fade's all messed up." She continued playing with the thing, and I had to admit that the sound was becoming remarkably better. Satisfied, she sat back in the seat, even going so far as to hold out her other hand for Dog to sniff. He did and then licked her wrist.

"I love singer/storytellers." She scratched under the beast's chin and for the first time since I'd met her seemed to relax as she listened to the lyrics. "You know this song is a joke, right? He wrote it in response to the uninformed view of the Vietnam War. He said he figured it was what his dad would've thought."

I shrugged noncommittally.

She stared at the side of my face, possibly at my ear or the lack of a tiny bit of it. "Were you over there?"

I nodded.

"So was my dad." Her eyes went back to the road. "That's why I'm going home; he died."

I navigated my way around a string of slow-moving cars. "What did your father do?"

Her voice dropped to a trademark baritone, buttery and resonant. "KERR, 750 AM. Polson, Montana."

I laughed. "I thought you didn't do AM."

"Yeah, well, now you know why."

Merle swung into "Pancho and Lefty," and she pointed to the stereo. "Proof positive that he *did* smoke marijuana in Muskogee — he's friends with Willie Nelson."

I raised an eyebrow. "In my line of work, we call that guilt by association."

"Yeah, well, in my line of work, we call it a friggin' fact — Willie's smoked like a Cummins diesel everywhere, including Muskogee, Oklahoma."

I had to concede the logic. "You seem to know a lot about the industry. Nashville?"

"Yeah."

"Okay, so you're not a musician. What did you do?"

"Still do, when I get through in Polson." Her eyes went back to the windshield and her future. "Produce, audio engineer . . . Or I try to." She nibbled on one of the nails, on the hand that held the shiny cup. "Did you know that less than 5 percent of producers and engineers in the business are women?" I waited, but she seemed preoccupied, finally sipping her coffee again and then pouring herself another. "We're raised to be attractive and accommodating, but we're not raised to know our shit and stand by it." She was quiet for a while, listening to the lyrics. "Townes Van Zandt wrote that one. People think it's about Pancho Villa, but one of the lines is about him getting hung — Pancho Villa was gunned down."

I nodded and glanced at her lap. "Seven men standing in the road in Hidalgo del Parral shot more than forty rounds into his roadster."

"You worked for the History Channel before you were sheriff?" I didn't say anything, and the smile lingered on her face like fingerpicking on a warped-neck fretboard. "You're okay-looking, in a dad kind of way."

I widened my eyes. "That's a disturbing statement for a number of reasons."

She barked a laugh and raised one of the combat boots up to lodge it against the transmission hump, but realized she was revealing the pistol from the drape of the blanket on her lap and lowered her foot. "My dad never talked about it, Vietnam . . . He handled that Agent Orange stuff and that shit gave robots cancer." Her eyes were drawn back to the windshield and Polson. "He died last week and they're already splitting up his stuff." The mile markers clicked by like the wand on a metronome. "He taught me how to listen — I mean really listen. To hear things that nobody else heard. He had this set of Sennheiser HD414 open-back headphones from '73, lightweight with the first out-of-head imaging with decent bass — Sony Walkmans and all that stuff should get down and kiss Sennheiser's ass. They had a steel cord and you could throw them at a *talented* program director or a brick wall — I'm not sure which is potentially denser."

It was an unsettling tirade, but I still had to laugh.

"You don't have any idea what I'm talking about, do you?"

"Nope, but it all sounds very impressive." We topped the hill above Billings and looked at the lit-up refineries that ran along the highway as I made the sweeping turn west, the power of internal combustion pushing us back in the leather seats like we were tobogganing down a hill. The tires ran silent and floated on a cushion of air headlong into the snowy dunes and shimmering lights strung alongside the highway like fuzzy moons.

She turned away, keeping her eyes from me, afraid that I might see too much there. "You can just drop me at the Golden Pheasant; I've got friends doing a gig who'll give me a ride the rest of the way."

Nodding, I joined with the linear constellation of I-94.

I had a vague sense of the club's location downtown, took the Twenty-seventh Street exit, rolled past the Montana Women's Prison and the wrong side of the railroad tracks, and then sat there watching the hundred and fifty coal cars of a Burlington

Northern Santa Fe train roll by.

When she finally spoke, her voice was different, saner. "It belonged to my father. When I was leaving for Tennessee, he gave me a choice of those headphones I was telling you about, but I figured I'd have more use for the gun." She placed her hand on the dash and fingered the vent louvers as the two of us looked at the plastic strip on her wrist. "I got in some trouble down there." Her voice died in her throat, but after a moment she started again. "I got picked up by a few guys over in South Dakota earlier tonight and they tried stuff. They seemed nice at first . . ." She gestured with the pistol, still under the blanket. "Anyway, I had to pull it."

I turned down a side street and took a right, where I could see the multicolored neon of the aforementioned pheasant spreading his tail feathers in a provocative manner. I parked the truck in the first available spot and turned to look at the girl with the strange eyes, the sifting snow providing a surreal scrim to her backlit face.

"I didn't shoot anybody."

"Good."

She smiled and finished the dregs of her coffee, wiped the cup out on her blanket, and screwed the top back on the thermos.

She placed it against the console, but the movement caused the revolver to slip from her leg and onto the seat between us.

We both sat there looking at it, representative of all the things for which it stood.

I leaned forward and picked it up. It had been a nice one once upon a time, but years of negligence had left it scuffed and rusted, emerald corrosion growing from the rounds permanently imbedded in the cylinder. "How 'bout I keep this for you?"

She didn't say anything for a long time but finally slipped through the open door, pulled the guitar case from the bed of my truck, and stood there in the opening.

The plaintive words of Haggard's "A Place to Fall Apart" drifted from the speakers, and she glanced at the radio as if the Okie from wherever might be sitting on my dash. "I'd give a million dollars if he'd go into a studio, just him and a six-string guitar, no backup singers, no harps — and just play."

I watched her face, trying not to let the eyes distract me. "Maybe you should tell him that sometime, but I wouldn't look for him in Muskogee."

The wind pressed the blanket against her, urging departure, and I was struck by the sudden vulnerability in her face as she closed the door, the words barely audible:

"Merry Christmas."

She continued to clutch the blanket around her as she turned. Dragging the guitar case, she walked away without looking back and disappeared into the swinging glass doors with swirls of snow devils circling after her; all I could think was that I was glad I wasn't in Polson, Montana, and in possession of a set of Sennheiser HD414 open-back headphones.

I thought about the things you could do, and the things you couldn't, even in a season of miracles.

I tossed the decrepit revolver into my glove box, sure that whoever might have pulled the trigger on the thing had as equal a chance of getting hurt as the person at whom it was being pointed.

Twenty minutes later, my daughter climbed in the cab. "Please tell me we're not staying at the Dude Rancher."

I smiled, and she pulled the shoulder belt around in a huff as Merle softened his tone with one of my favorites, "If We Make It Through December."

She ruffled Dog's hair and kissed his muzzle, and it must've taken a good thirty seconds before she remarked, "Did you get a new stereo in the truck, Dad? It sounds really good."

# SEVERAL STATIONS

*"Many calls that night, did Scrooge make with the Spirit of Christmas Present. Down among the miners who labored in the bowels of the earth. And out to sea among the sailors at their watch, dark, ghostly figures and their several stations."*

"What do you want to do, Sheriff?"

I paused, repeating the lines in my head, and glanced at the young Wyoming highway patrolman. I envied him his insulated coveralls — mine were still folded up behind the seat of my truck. I ducked my head down and peered around the flipped-up collar of my sheepskin coat and from under the brim of my hat.

The highway patrol had closed the interstate and the driver of the big eighteen-wheeler had negotiated the off-ramp but had only gotten as far as the first turn on the Durant county road before he slid off and slowly rolled the truck over like an apatosaurus looking to make a giant snow angel. "Go home, troop."

The emergency lights from his cruiser were flashing, and the both of us turned blue and red like a rotating color wheel on a Christmas tree as he shook his head. "I'll stick around and —"

"Go home. I'm sure that family of yours in Sheridan would like to see you sometime before Christmas day." We'd been talking while the EMTs checked the rather nonplussed truck driver, who said the insurance would cover the damages. He didn't appear injured, but they'd hauled him away to Durant Memorial as a precaution.

The trooper had been transferred from the Evanston detachment and had been enjoying the new duty, at least up until tonight. He'd done a stint in the first Gulf War and was now married with three kids and trying to make it on state wages — he didn't mention which was tougher. I looked out toward the closed highway across a landscape that, if it didn't look like the North Pole, was getting very close to looking like Barrow, Alaska. "You don't get going soon, you might not make it."

He glanced back at his two-wheel-drive Interceptor — good for a hundred and forty miles an hour on dry pavement and in current conditions good for about twenty. "What about you, don't you have people?"

I looked back at my snow-covered truck and nodded toward Dog, who I could see through the sweeping windshield wipers was sitting in the passenger seat. "My only in-town family this holiday." I pushed his shoulder toward his unit but not so hard that he'd slip. "Go."

He looked at me, then at the overturned tractor and sheared-open trailer with its contents scattered across the snowy ditch. "Thanks."

"You bet."

"And Merry Christmas, Walt."

I watched as he got into his vehicle, carefully executed the three-point turn, and disappeared, making a tunnel in the suspended flakes.

Over the last two days, we'd had blizzard conditions with twenty-four inches of snow, forty-mile-an-hour gusts, and a visibility of about a quarter mile. The mercury hadn't risen above twelve degrees, and the last time I'd checked, it was fifteen below.

Maybe I'd put my coveralls on after all.

I started the long trudge toward Saizarbi-toria, who was driving Vic's vehicle while she was in Philadelphia for the holidays because it had four-wheel drive. The second unit of the Absaroka County Sheriff's Department was parked at the other end of the inverted behemoth.

The way the eighteen-wheeler had landed, the back end of the trailer had remained flat, while the culverts had twisted the front and torn the thin metal sides. It was as if some giant had picked the thing up and pulled at it from both ends like a holiday cracker. Along the sides were painted the words TOYS-R-US.

NOT-2-NIGHT-U-R-NOT.

I tugged my hat down and pulled open the door of our eight-year-old unit. Dragging my coat in behind me, I closed the door. Saizarbitoria was talking on his phone. ". . . No, he was really good and he knew his line — once he got started."

Evidently he was talking to Vic, who wanted to know how last night's Durant Community Theater production of *A Christmas Carol* had gone. The varsity basketball player who was supposed to play the Ghost of Christmas Future had come down with something, probably nerves, and had left the production in the lurch. I was the only one that Mary Jo, the director, could think of who was tall enough, so I'd been called in to play the role. I had accepted only when she assured me that it wasn't a speaking

110

part; I would just have to point. She hadn't mentioned that I had to wear a floor-length black robe with a hood and that all of my scenes would be done in the dark.

Then, in a fit of apology, she'd given me a line that had belonged to the young man, a part of a voice-over narrative passage from the middle of the play.

Ian McKellen would've wept.

"Here, you can ask him yourself." The Basquo handed me the phone.

I held the device a little away from my ear, a lesson learned after having communicated with my undersheriff in like manner before. "What?"

"I heard you almost crushed Scrooge."

I sighed. "I only slipped once."

"I heard he had to help you up."

I cleared my throat "Just a little."

"You don't think that kind of blew the fucking concept — Scrooge helping death up off the floor?"

I felt the blood rising in my face. "We made it work."

"I heard the audience laughed their asses off."

I glanced at Sancho and wondered what else he'd told her. I pulled a glove and held my fingers in front of the vent in the dash, which was blowing life-giving warmth.

"There were a few chuckles."

I listened to the sounds of the not-so-silent night between Wyoming and Philadelphia. "Look, I know it was live theater and you have to allow for a certain amount of improvisation, but contrary to popular belief, people aren't supposed to laugh in the face of death."

"Sure they are."

"Let me hear your one line."

I cleared my throat and recited, *"Many calls that night, did Scrooge make with the Spirit of Christmas Present. Down among the miners who labored in the bowels of the earth. And out to sea among the sailors at their watch, dark, ghostly figures and their several stations."*

There was a long pause. "Not exactly *'God bless us, every one.'* "

Everybody's a critic and, even with my limited theatrical experience, I felt the need to stand up for my singular contribution to the play. "It's a good line."

"What the hell does it mean?"

I could feel the nerves reawakening in my hand as I considered. "I think Dickens was saying something about the people who have to work through the holidays, and how the spirit of Christmas is always there, doing what it's supposed to do no matter

what, reminding people of their humanity."
She didn't have a smart-aleck response for
that, but I waited the requisite three seconds
before changing the subject anyway. "How's
your family?"

I imagined her lips pursing as she blew
into the phone. "I haven't gotten over there
yet."

"You've been in the city for two days, and
it's Christmas Eve."

Her voice took on a familiar edge, sharp-
ening as it always did when she talked about
her family. "I'm working on it, all right?"

I glanced over at Santiago and then back
to the phone as if I expected to see her face.
"Okay."

After a few moments, she spoke again. "I
heard you had a slider."

I looked through the windshield at the
crumpled truck and trailer as the wipers
slapped another eighth of an inch of snow
off the glass. "Yep, I was just getting ready
to send everybody home when the HPs
called it in."

"Just you and Sancho on?"

"Yep." I glanced at the young man, who
looked like one of Dumas' musketeers. "I
sent the Ferg home along with Ruby and
told the Gold Dust Twins that they could
shut down the Powder River Junction de-

tachment at four."

"Where's Henry?"

"Disappeared, for the moment." I yawned, in spite of myself. "I'm planning on sending Sancho off here in a few minutes." He started to speak, but I held up a warmed hand and silenced him. "Why don't you call me back later?"

I listened as she readjusted the receiver. "You're sleeping at the jail?"

"Eventually . . ." The gusts rocked the vehicle. "Call me back later, okay?"

"Yeah, hey?"

I waited. "Yep?"

". . . I miss you."

I glanced back at Saizarbitoria as he occupied himself with the accident reports clipped on his aluminum board and attempted to keep the drops from his thawing facial hair from hitting the paper. "I miss you, too." It was quiet on the phone, then I heard a soft click and she was gone. I handed my deputy his cell back and watched as he snapped it shut and tucked it behind the embroidered star on the breast pocket of his coveralls. "What'd the wrecker say?"

He shook his head. "Not for another forty-five minutes at least."

I checked the distance between us and my vehicle. "Does Vic have any of those emergency beacons in the back with the flares?"

He thought about it. "Yeah, the yellow ones on the sawhorses."

I nodded. "I'll tell you what, set one up next to the guardrail, tie it off with a couple of those rubber straps, and give me a few more flares for the roadside — then you go home."

He shook his head. "No, I'll just wait with —"

"Don't be stupid, you've got a wife with child, and this night is notorious for the miraculous arrival of children."

"What if you get another call?"

I nudged the mic on his dash with my knee. "We haven't had another call in over an hour, and, with the way it's coming down, anybody in their right mind is at home, in bed, with visions of sugarplums dancing in their heads."

He looked at me. "What is a sugarplum, anyway?"

I pulled my gloves on. "It's a plum, with sugar on it — I'm speaking from a purely onomasiological basis."

He nodded, and we both got out. He handed me the extra flares and left to secure the one at the guardrail, and I began tromping my way along the bypass, tasting the sulfur as I dropped them on top of the ones

115

we'd lit earlier, now smoldering and dying.

By the time I got back to my vehicle, I'd made the decision to put on my winter gear. I pulled the coveralls from behind my seat and felt around for my rubber overboots; then I tossed everything onto the seat cover that my daughter had given me for Christmas last year.

Dog sat in the passenger seat beside the gift that Cady had sent this year, the special one that could be opened on Christmas Eve. It was a tradition that had started when she was just a little girl and I had given her a special dress that she could wear to her grandparents' house the day before Christmas, because I knew that she could never wait for the opportunity to sport new clothes.

I peeled off my coat and stuffed it in the back, flipped my hat onto the dash, and hung my duty belt on the steering wheel. I quickly unzipped the front, legs, and sleeves of the coveralls, and then stepped in and zipped them the rest of the way up.

Snow was blowing past me into the cab as I pulled on the overboots and latched the clasps. I reached for my hat and spoke to Dog, who watched me the way his kind had always watched my kind from just outside the light of our fires. "I know you need to get out, but let me get everything settled and then I'll take you for a short walk. Okay?" He didn't say anything but curled around and settled with his head on the small cardboard box postmarked from Old City, Philadelphia.

I took the Maglite and a radio from my Sam Browne but left the rest of my equipment on the belt, including my .45 Colt; I was pretty sure there wasn't going to be any gunplay tonight. I checked the frequency on the handheld, adjusted the volume, and deposited it in my inside breast pocket, the rubber antenna pressing against my neck. I slipped the flashlight in the long pocket along my thigh and gave Dog one last look. "I promise."

I discovered my insulated winter gloves in the pockets of my Carhartts, tugged them on, and drew the wrist cinch straps tight as Santiago pulled Vic's unit alongside my truck, which I had dubbed the Bullet. I got out, slammed the door behind me, and pulled my hat down. The gusts almost took it again, so I pulled it down tighter, wishing I'd remembered to order those cowboy ear mufflers with the stampede strings that would have kept the ever-prevalent Wyoming wind from carrying my headgear to Nebraska, or turning my ears to jerky.

Sancho didn't even bother with the window, since they had long since stopped working in the blizzard; instead, he cracked the door open, which sounded like a glacier splitting. "You're sure about this?"

"If I need you, I'll call you; it's only forty-five minutes. What could happen?" He studied me until I raised my arm slowly, my index finger pointed toward town like the ghostly specter I'd portrayed the night before. *"Many calls that night, did Scrooge make with the Spirit of Christmas Present. Down among the miners who labored in the bowels of the earth. And out to sea among the sailors at their watch, dark, ghostly figures and their several stations."*

"Bravo." He smiled through the ice in his Vandyke and mimed clapping his hands. The effervescence had returned to his eyes, and he slowly shook his head. "Merry Christmas, boss." He shut the door and slowly drove back up the road toward town.

I stayed in character till the coast was clear and then carefully made my way around the truck in the continuous blue strobe of the light bar. I opened the door, and Dog leapt from the cab into the wind-sculpted drifts. I watched as he took a great mouthful and ate it, deigning to return to the side of the truck only long enough to give it the one-leg salute. As he prowled the ditch and sniffed the few boxes that were scattered between the Bullet and the wrecked trailer, I leaned against the front fender and thought about my performance.

In over a quarter century of law enforcement, I'd faced about every type of intimidating situation I could imagine, but nothing had prepared me for the moment when I took those six steps to the center of the Durant Playhouse's stage and, in the glare of the lights and under public scrutiny, attempted to deliver the three sentences I'd been repeating for the previous forty-eight hours.

Like a mule deer in the headlights, I'd opened my mouth and nothing had come out.

Another gust showered me with the frozen shards that had blown from the hood of my truck and carried my hat into the ditch a good ten yards away. "Well, hell . . ." I looked at Dog, who was investigating about halfway between my hat and me, raised my ghostly gloved finger, and pointed at the quivering piece of beaver felt, which was threatening to blow even further away. "Fetch."

He sat.

I sighed and trying not to allow too much

snow to climb up my pant legs into my over-boots started down the hillside. Dog leapt from his sitting position and made a playful grab at my hand — he must have thought that I'd climbed down in the ditch to play. I swatted him once and then felt him mouth my glove in his teeth until my hand grew numb. "Hey." He let go and looked sheep-ish, or at least as sheepish as an animal that looked like a cross between a bear and wolf can look.

I was within a step from my hat when the wind kicked it over again and blew it against one of the boxes that had spilled from the truck. I felt the sweat hardening in my hair as I post-holed my way through the next drift and rescued the 10X before it could take off again.

Figuring I could assist in the cleanup that would hopefully commence within the hour, I leaned down and picked up the carton, brushed off the snow, and read the label along with the model number — UB-742.

I lodged it under my arm and retraced the holes in the snowpack that I had made, this time up the hillside, just in time to see a pair of headlights slowly making their way around the bypass curve and creeping even slower down the road in the face of the emergency lights.

From the configuration of the grille, I could tell it wasn't Saizarbitoria.

When I got back to the edge of the road, I raised my hand in greeting to the people in the old Toyota 4Runner with a bashed-in fender. They were going slow enough to be safe, but they slowed even more when they saw me, and finally came to a stop.

Dog joined me as I stepped around the corner of my truck and stooped down to look in the driver's-side window. It was rolled down about four inches, but the young man who had been driving kept his eyes on the road. Next to him was a child bundled up in a blanket and a young woman who leaned across the toddler and screamed at me, "Where the hell are we supposed to go?!"

Assuming I must've lost the first part of the conversation, I moved in closer and balanced the package on my hip. "Excuse me?"

She looked disgusted and then began yelling again. "We tried to get on the highway and you wouldn't let us, now we're trying to get home and you won't even let us do that!"

I glanced at the man, who remained immobile. I guessed he'd done his part in the Christmas Eve shouting match before I'd arrived and was now leaving the rest to me.

I could've just let it go and waved them on, but there are times when you feel the need to do a little social work. I set the box down by my boots. "License, registration, and proof of insurance."

The woman, whom I assumed was his wife, threw herself back against the seat in a fit of pique and folded her arms. "I don't believe this."

The driver dug out his paperwork and handed it to me through the slim opening without meeting my eyes. I pulled the Maglite from the leg of my coveralls and focused its beam on his license. His name was Leonard Trice, and he lived about a mile down the road. "Mr. Trice, do you mind if I ask what you're doing out on a night like this?"

The woman leaned back across him and the child, who was now awake and howling. She spoke slowly and loudly, as if I didn't speak English. "We were on our way over to Sheridan for some last minute shopping, but you closed the highway!"

She said it as if we'd done it to spite her. "Mrs. Trice, the highway patrol has closed the roads from Hardin to Wheatland — there isn't anything open."

Now even she wasn't looking at me.

I studied the two of them and the crying

child, who was not in a car seat. I thought about how hard it had been for my wife and me when we'd started a family; how we'd scrimped and saved, and how it'd always seemed to take everything we had just to get by. I handed the man back his information. "Hold on just a sec."

I pulled the back door of the SUV open with a yank that quickly dislodged it from the ice, placed the box on the seat, and then closed the door with a solid thump. Looking down at him, I stood there in the blowing snow. "Merry Christmas."

He glanced into his backseat and then turned to look at me for the first time. "What's in it?"

I shrugged. "UB-742s, a whole carton of them." He continued to look at me. "It fell out of a sleigh."

He studied me for a moment longer. "Does that mean we can go?"

I couldn't, for the life of me, think of anything else to say, so I just pointed again and intoned: *Many calls that night, did Scrooge make with the Spirit of Christmas Present. Down among the miners who labored in the bowels of the earth. And out to sea among the sailors at their watch, dark, ghostly figures and their several stations.*

They all three stared at me. Then the

young man closed the window, and the family, without another word, pulled away in their battered Toyota.

All in all, I'd say it was a stunning performance.

I figured at this rate, if I kept practicing, I'd be ready for next year.

# High Holidays

We have a problem in northern Wyoming, the part between the Bighorn Mountains and Yellowstone National Park, that I call "people having been driven to distraction." Our state is host to roughly twelve million visitors a year, and it makes for a few problems, particularly for those of us in law enforcement.

We have our share of people who drive off the road because they are mesmerized by the first view of the snowcapped peaks, and those who try and pet the bears, ride the buffalo, or skinny-dip in the thermal pools.

Strangers in a strange land, tourists are prone to these kinds of mistakes, as well as to crimes of a more banal variety, like, say, driving off without paying for the gas they just bought.

The drive-off is the most prevalent unlawful act in the area, and it falls to those of us in either the Absaroka County Sheriff's

Department or the Wyoming Highway Patrol to pull the folks over and inform them that they owe the Kum & Go $47.63. I guess it could be worse.

Generally people turn bright red, at which point we give them a blue warning ticket and ask them to return to the station and pay the green. Sometimes people are broke and don't have the money, but usually folks are happy to return with the officer and pay up, and the service stations don't press charges — no harm, no foul.

It was one of those beautiful September afternoons when I happened to come upon Santiago Saizarbitoria out on the bypass. Sancho had detained a maroon Chrysler Town & Country pulling, appropriately enough, a U-Haul trailer adorned with the visage of state favorite Buffalo Bill, and emblazoned with the words CENTER OF THE WEST — CODY, GATEWAY TO YELLOWSTONE NATIONAL PARK.

Few traffic stops in Absaroka County are worthy of the attention of two officers, but I was on my way back from a Saturday morning DARE talk with the bored detention students at the Durant High School, so I slid the Bullet in beside the Basquo's unit and rolled down the window. "What's up, troop?"

Without looking at me, he gestured with a pen toward the vehicle in front of him. "Drive-off from the Maverik convenience store."

I glanced at the occupants. "I guess they decided it was convenient not to pay?"

"They seem harmless enough." He shrugged and looked at them. "I think they're Amish."

I ignored his attitude — he and his wife had been having a time with their son, Antonio, who, although he was approaching his first birthday, still had his own ideas about regular sleeping patterns. "How's life at home?"

He sighed. "I figure I'm getting about four hours of sleep a night and it's killing me. I thought by now he'd be easier."

My mind wandered to my daughter, The Greatest Legal Mind of Our Time. "Cady had colic one time and put Martha and me through the ringer; I know Vietnam POW friends of mine who didn't have to go through that kind of sleep deprivation."

Nodding, he continued to write up the warning ticket for the driver of the minivan. "I mean, I love him, but at two o'clock in the morning I feel like disciplining him with a weedwacker." He glanced at the back of the trailer in front of him and then read from the license on his clipboard. "Jacob Aaron of Nogales, Arizona."

I thought about the town on the Arizona border about a mile from Mexico. "Strange place to be Amish."

"Maybe they're rebel Amish, like those Hutterites in Montana — you know, the ones in the Big Horn valley who drive cars and have cell phones."

"Most of those are up in Alberta and Saskatchewan." I thought about it. "Did you know that they were persecuted during World War I, because they refused to fight? Four of them were imprisoned and two were killed in Leavenworth."

He turned to look at me. "I was joking, boss."

"Oh."

Yawning, he gestured toward the Chrysler. "You want me to follow them back to the gas station?"

I glanced at the vehicle, but I couldn't get a clear view of the passengers. "Well, if they're men of God, I think we can trust them to drive the half mile back and pay for the gas."

He shrugged and continued writing. "You're the boss, boss."

I pulled the three-quarter-ton down into gear. "When you get off duty, get some rest." Inching forward, I stopped by the driver's-side window to chat with the bearded, darkly clad driver. "Sorry we had to pull you over, Mr. Aaron."

He looked worried and even went so far as to take off his hat. "No, it's my fault." He gestured toward the man in the passenger seat. "Joseph went inside to get sandwiches and drinks and I thought he had paid for the gas."

Joseph looked sullen, took another bite of his sandwich, and chewed through the words. "I thought you paid."

I glanced behind them at the two in the back, who were similarly dressed. "On holiday?"

"Yes. We are seeing the Black Hills today. Hopefully."

"It should be beautiful that way with the aspens and cottonwoods changing color."

He nodded. "We hope so."

"Well, happy motoring."

I pulled the Bullet into reverse and backed up even with the Basquo. "They're Jewish."

He didn't look up. "Really."

"Yep. Hasidic, I'm guessing, from the dress and long sideburns."

The intonation of his response was exactly as before. "Really."

"You don't care."

He finally looked at me with red-rimmed eyes. "No, I don't."

"You know, part of the job is noticing things."

"Really."

"Like I said — get some rest." I nodded to myself, pulled the Bullet back into gear, and started off, calling out to him. "You've been hanging around with Vic too much."

Thinking about the high wise-guy quotient in my office, I drove past the lumberyard and noticed that I was low on gas, too.

Pulling into the Maverik, I slid the county card and began filling up my truck. As I stood there listening to "The Girl from Ipanema" piped in from the overhead speakers and trying to ignore the placard on the top of the pump touting sale prices on Rainier beer, I watched as the van with the Buffalo Bill U-Haul made a right on route 16 and headed east out of town.

I quickly clicked off the pump, hung it up, and called Santiago on my radio. "Hey, troop, did you just cut the guys with the U-Haul free?"

Static. "Yeah."

"Were they coming over here to pay for the gas?"

Static. "Yeah."

"Well, they just drove by the Maverik headed for the interstate like the Macy's Day parade."

Static. "You've got to be kidding."

I fired up the Bullet and pulled through the pump island onto the road with my light bar on but no siren. "Don't worry; I'll get 'em. They're probably lost."

With the Chrysler safely pulled over again, this time at the I-90 entrance ramp, I climbed out and walked toward them, passing Buffalo Bill and running my hand over the single row of shiny sheet-metal screws on the side of the trailer.

"Howdy again."

The man looked even more embarrassed this time. "We can't find the gas station."

I glanced down the road. "About a half mile back that way; it's across from where you pulled out." He turned and again gave an accusatory look at his passenger, who was eating from a bag of chips. "If you want, you can just follow me back."

He dipped his head. "Of course. Thank you."

I led them to the Maverik and watched as they parked in the shade next to the picnic tables beside Clear Creek. With a dark look, Joseph ducked past my truck, and went

131

inside. I got out, too, figuring what the hey, I'd take advantage of the Rainier sale and grab an eighteen-pack for Gameday. The Broncos-Chiefs game was tomorrow, so Henry would be over to watch — I would, as always, torment him with my beer of choice.

I set my prospective purchase on the counter and stood behind Joseph in line. "Don't forget to pay for those snacks along with the gas."

He nodded curtly. The kid at the register rang him up, and Joseph paid in cash from a wad secured with a thick rubber band.

"Enjoy the Hills."

He glanced up at me, nodded, and went out the door without a word. The cashier held his receipt out after him but finally dropped it on the counter. "Those Amish, they're weird."

I picked up the abandoned ticket and examined it.

They weren't as happy to see me this time, as I raised a hand to keep them from pulling away from the convenience store. "Mr. Aaron, I was wondering if I could ask you a few questions?"

He looked genuinely annoyed. "This is getting to be a bit much — I mean, we paid

132

for the gas. Is there another problem, Sheriff?"

"No, no, nothing like that. I just don't get the opportunity to discuss different theologies very often and was wondering if you could answer a few quick questions for me."

He glanced at the clock in the dash, avoided my eyes, and made a definitive statement by reaching down to turn the key and firing up the Chrysler. "We are hoping to be in the Black Hills today."

Ignoring the fact that the vehicle was running, I tipped my hat back and folded my arms on his window. "Oh, this won't take long — you're Hasidic, are you not?"

He nodded, quickly adding, "Yes we are, but . . ."

"I hope you'll excuse my ignorance, but the Hasidim are Haredi or ultra-Orthodox — one of the most conservative forms of Judaism, am I correct?"

"Well, yes."

"Now, the Hasidim wear clothing that other Orthodox Jews can't wear, such as the tallit katan over the shirts, like some of you gentlemen are wearing now, whereas other Orthodox Jews have to wear them under their shirts with only the tzitzit hanging out, right?"

He studied my face. "You . . . You seem

133

extraordinarily knowledgeable on the subject of Judaism for a Wyoming sheriff."

I smiled. "Well, I had a Jewish girlfriend in college, and you'd be surprised what you can learn when you're motivated, and with the right teacher."

Nervously, he turned to his compatriots and then stared at the wheel. "I see."

I reached out and patted his shoulder. "Oh, I'm just showing off . . . But I do have just one more question, if you don't mind."

He nodded again, but this time with even less enthusiasm as he looked in his side mirror and saw Saizarbitoria's unit pulling in behind him. "Uh . . . Anything we can do to help."

"Well, if the Hasidim are the most conservative of the Jewish Orthodoxy, how is it you're driving a car on the Sabbath?"

He inhaled and then took a very long time to look me in the eye. "Excuse me?"

"It's Saturday, Mr. Aaron, and even I know that it's forbidden. As one of the thirty-nine types of work the Torah prohibits on the Sabbath, isn't starting a car a form of lighting a fire? I mean, correct me if I'm wrong, but you hit the ignition, the engine burns the fuel . . ."

His mouth moved and finally something came out. "Oh, my . . . Umm. We've been traveling, and we must've lost track of the days." He reached down and turned off the ignition. "Thank you for reminding us."

"I know that some Orthodox and Reform Jews drive on the Sabbath for specific purposes such as going to synagogue, but the nearest ones are down in Cheyenne and up in Billings, and since you said, numerous times, that you were going to the Black Hills today . . ."

He cleared his throat and mumbled something unintelligible.

I reached in across the steering wheel, pulled the keys, and stuffed them in my jacket pocket to keep my hands free. "Also, not only does this happen to be a Saturday and the Sabbath, but it's also Rosh Hashanah."

His eyes grew very wide.

"Happy New Year, Mr. Aaron, it's the start of the high holidays." I adjusted my Ray-Bans and placed the web of my thumb onto the hammer of my .45 Colt. "The Day of Judgment is to come."

I glanced back and watched as Saizarbitoria stepped from his unit and, walking behind their trailer, came up on the passenger side. "In all honesty, I probably wouldn't have noticed myself, but it was on a holiday calendar up at the high school

135

where I was doing a DARE talk with some of the wayward students who had to come in for detention on a Saturday. DARE is the Drug Abuse Resistance Education program; I'm not sure if it does a lot of good, but it gives me a chance to go in and talk to the kids and maybe convince them that there are better ways to spend their time."

He didn't move.

"Rosh Hashanah is the pronouncement of the Day of Judgment as I recall, but it's not final until Yom Kippur, so you get ten days to alter your behavior, correct?"

"Um, yes."

I moved back, pulled the handle on his door, and swung it wide. "How about stepping out here with me for a moment?"

Sitting there with his seat belt still attached, I guess he was gauging his options, but there really wasn't any way out. Slowly, he unfastened the belt and turned, sliding from the vehicle as the man in the passenger seat reached down for something in the glove compartment.

Sancho's Beretta .40 lodged behind Joseph's right ear, his voice as cool and calm as a loaded number 6 bear trap. "Sheriff's department — don't you move."

I walked the driver back to the U-Haul and thumped a forefinger on Buffalo Bill's

136

studded chest. "You see this extra set of sheet-metal screws up near the bulkhead, Mr. Aaron?"

He nodded his head and then dropped it to study his shoes.

"There's no paint on them, which leads me to believe that they were added after the others, possibly to provide a hidden cavity within the trailer." I stepped back and measured the cargo space with my eyes. "Now, I'm guessing, but from the dimensions, I'd say it's probably close to two hundred pounds of marijuana in there, which means you and your friends are facing felony charges of possession of a controlled substance, possession of a controlled substance with intent to deliver, and conspiracy with intent to deliver a controlled substance to the tune of well over a million dollars street value."

The Basquo brought the other men around the van and had them leaning against the side with their fingers laced behind their heads and their legs spread wide, a Glock 19 with rubber bands wrapped around the handle lodged in the back of his duty belt.

I turned the driver toward the U-Haul, his head against the sheet metal, with Buffalo Bill, our blue-eyed boy, looking down at him in haughty disdain. "You know, Mr. Aaron . . ." I attached the cuffs to his wrists and turned him around, smiling at him sadly. "You might've gotten away with it if your friend hadn't bought the ham sandwich and the bag of pork rinds."

# TOYS FOR TOTS

She has always enjoyed pushing buttons; I think she got it from her mother, who was always quick to punch the ones in elevators. She likes gadgets — phones, cameras, computers — anything with buttons.

I said nothing as she adjusted the heater higher and turned the louvers in the vent toward herself, closing her eyes and savoring the warmth. The windshield wipers, set on automatic, slapped across the glass three times.

"Gimme your gun."

"Why?"

"I wanna shoot you."

With more than a quarter-century in law enforcement, I'm savvy to the ways of criminals and emotionally disturbed people. "No."

She'd just arrived from Philadelphia, and we were driving down from the Billings airport to the town proper on the winding

Zimmerman Trail. It was close to Christmas, and my daughter needed things. Cady pulled a few strands of strawberry blond hair from her face with a bright grin. "So . . . I'll ask again, what do you want for the holidays?"

"I don't need anything."

She turned in the seat and, refusing to dim the cheer, reached back and scratched the fur behind Dog's ears. He grinned, too. "That — is *not* what I asked."

I navigated the intersection at Grand and Twenty-seventh Street. "I'd rather you saved your money." I slowed the truck and watched the first snowflakes drift innocently down from the darkened sky, the way they always did; we were two hours from home across some of the emptiest high plains countryside, and I wasn't fooled. "Do we have to go to the mall?"

Three more slaps of the wipers.

Cady's clear, frank, gray eyes traveled across the defrosting windshield in my direction with a frost of their own. "You are not adopting the proper gift-purchasing and gift-giving attitude." She let that statement settle before continuing. "No, we don't have to go to the mall; but if you could run me down to Gillette, I'd like to get you a ton of bulk product for Christmas."

Gillette, Wyoming — with one of the largest open-pit coal mines in the world.

"A week ago, you said we could do some shopping when you picked me up."

I did.

"You promised."

I had.

She stretched out a hand, the sleeve of her Burberry coat riding up her arm, and flipped on the radio, readjusting the station to "Grandma Got Run Over by a Reindeer." "You always get like this at the holidays." She fooled with the search button, this time coming up with Andy Williams and "It's the Most Wonderful Time of the Year." "What's the best gift Mom ever gave you?"

"You."

Three slaps.

"Besides me."

I thought about it but couldn't really come up with anything. I added, as an afterthought, "She bought me these Peerless stainless-steel handcuffs that are on my belt."

"I'm not buying you handcuffs for Christmas." She pulled the visor down, sliding open the hidden mirror I always forgot was there, and smoothed her lip gloss with her index finger. "What about your radio?"

I glanced at my dash and Andy Williams.

"What's wrong with my radio?"

Cady snapped her reflection shut and flipped the visor up with a wave of her hand. "The one at home, the weather thingamajiggie."

"The NOAA radio?"

She reinforced the thought by pointing at me with the finger that was smudged with the lip gloss residue.

She was right — the thing had died. Everyone on the high plains has one — they pick up the frequency of the National Oceanic and Atmospheric Administration so that their owners can find out just how many feet of snow are going to be on the ground in the morning.

Dog had knocked the device from the counter, at which point it had stopped receiving the local alerts. I had finalized its demise with a Phillips screwdriver, when I had attempted to take it apart on my kitchen table while talking to my daughter long distance. "It died."

She nodded in exasperation. "I know; you said you killed it."

I glanced back at Dog. "It was natural causes."

"So you *need* another one." She emphasized the word with a smile.

I really didn't; I'd gotten out of the habit

of listening to it after Henry alerted me to the fact that I had a tendency to leave it on for hours at a time. I still suspected the Cheyenne Nation of moving the radio close to the edge of the counter where Dog could get tangled in the cord. The Bear had his own ways of knowing the weather and, better yet, which way the wind blew.

"I guess I do, then."

Excited, she nudged forward on the truck seat. "Where do you buy them?"

"Radio Shack."

"Where's Radio Shack?"

"The mall."

Three slaps.

I'd ended up successfully avoiding the Rimrock Mall by suggesting that we go to one of the big-box stores instead. I parked the Bullet beside a light post in the parking lot of the Best Buy. Cady slipped out the passenger side as I opened the suicide door and let Dog out onto the snow-dusted grass berm to relieve himself.

She came around the truck and stood with me, her arm linked with mine. Cady watched Dog lift his leg on the candy-striped lamppost, and I leaned against the fender, drew her closer to me, and studied the lights of the MasterLube across the way.

What I really needed was to get the oil changed in my truck — I was a good four hundred miles over.

"I'm not buying you an oil change for Christmas, either."

I looked at her as she watched Dog. With her eyes glistening and the flakes resting gently on her hair like a blessing, she looked so much like her mother that I had to catch my breath. "You . . ." I bit the vapor escaping from my lungs along with my words.

She looked up at me. "What is it? Mom?"

I glanced away and lifted up my hat, scratched the hair underneath, and then lodged it back on. "I don't know . . . I guess."

She nodded and bumped her hip into mine, pulling in even closer against me. She squirmed her way into the crook and draped my arm over her shoulder. "I miss her, too."

"I know you do."

"But you need to get with the Christmas program, Daddy."

"I know."

She sighed against my chest, and I could feel the words welling up in her. "Dad, I may not be coming home for the holidays as much anymore. I've kind of got my own life back East, and I'm thinking I'd rather use the time off from the firm in the summer."

I thought about Vic's younger brother, the Philadelphia patrolman who had asked my daughter for her hand and pretty much everything else. "Sure."

"If this is our last Christmas alone together, I was thinking that it would be nice if it was a good one."

"Uh-huh."

Her head shifted past the thick collar of my sheepskin coat, where she could watch Dog. "That's one long pee."

I watched as he gave out with the last few surges. "He saves it up for when you come home."

Dog, aware that we were talking about him, broke off the irrigation and came over to poke his muzzle jealously between us. Cady turned her face up and stood on tiptoe, grazing her glossed lips against my stubble.

"I'm probably going to get some things for some of the other people on my list, too, so I would appreciate it if you would brighten your mood and come in and help me carry in a little while. All right?"

Dog and I watched her twirl her black greatcoat, fling her cha-cha fun fur, tinsel-threaded scarf over her shoulder, and march between the parked cars of the Best Buy parking lot as if it were the steppes of Russia.

I looked down at him. "Show-off."

Smiling and wagging, he looked up at me. "Yep. Laugh now. PetSmart is right next door, and I bet she'll want to get you a pair of those reindeer antlers with the jingle bells."

After loading the beast back into the truck, I stood there for a minute. I really didn't want to go in yet. The air was bracing, and maybe that's what I needed, a little slap in the face. I stood there for a while, watching the cars wheel in and out of the parking lot and hoping my mood would shift like the traffic.

I remembered the first Christmas with Cady and how she'd refused to go to bed — the life of the party at eight months. Martha and I had had a Christmas picnic by candlelight on a Hudson's Bay blanket we had thrown on the floor beside the crib. It was the best Christmas dinner I ever remember having.

Glancing at my profile in the side window of my truck, the flakes clinging to the mirror and blocking my inspection just enough so that I could stand the view, I gave the hard eye to the man who had been left tackle of the almost-national-champion University of Southern California Trojans, to the First Division Marine investigator, and to the man who was now the high sheriff of Absaroka County — informing him, in no uncertain terms, that it was time he straighten up and fly right.

He didn't seem overly impressed, so I took him for a walk.

The parking lot was crowded near the entrance of the electronics store, with the lights spilling from the whooshing pneumatic doors and the trumpeting of classic holiday music thundering against the heavy glass where stickers held a large red and white December calendar informing the world that only three days of shopping remained before Christmas.

I ambled through the empty handicapped spots and around a forest-green Wrangler toward the concrete pillars that kept the populace from parking inside the store. My eyes shifted past the calendar to a lean young man in a Navy dress uniform and an arm sling. He stood by a large cardboard box that had been covered with gold- and silver-foil wrapping paper, on top of which was pasted a red toy train logo carrying the words TOYS FOR TOTS.

As an inactive Marine — because there is no such thing as an ex-Marine — I was intimate with the program; in fact, I had manned the bin in front of Buell's hardware store myself on numerous Christmases back home in Durant.

The charity had been started by Marine reservist Major Will Hendricks back in '47 when his wife couldn't find an organization that would give a doll that she had made to a needy child. Along with being a Marine reservist, Hendricks had also been a director of public relations for Warner Brothers and had used his considerable influence to place bins to collect used toys outside movie theaters.

Decades later, when giving out hand-me-downs had become controversial, collections had been switched to include only new toys. In the nineties, the secretary of defense had approved Toys for Tots as an official mission of the Marine Corps Reserve.

I made eye contact with the young Navy chaplain. "You get drafted?"

He grinned. "We minister to the Marines, and since I'm on medical leave I'm considered an unofficial reservist." I looked down at his right sleeve and could see the small cross above the arm bands. He dipped his head a little, going so far as to loosen the sling at his chest to reveal the collar underneath his uniform jacket. He looked up at me under the patent leather of his dress lid. "Semper Fi?"

I spread my gloved hands. "Ours is not to question why."

He stuck out his own. "Ensign Gene Burch."

We shook. "Lieutenant Walt Longmire."

"Whoa." He saluted and studied me closer. "Vietnam, Lieutenant?"

" '67–'68. You?"

"Afghanistan."

I glanced at the front of the store as the door swept open and a young couple exited with numerous bags; I stepped to the right and positioned myself out of the way. The chaplain gave the pair a smile, but having put nothing in the box, they ducked aside quickly, embarrassed at their lack of largess.

I shuffled my boots in the snow. "That must've been fun."

He nodded. "Until I dislocated my shoulder and they sent me back home on medical leave."

I studied him a little closer and pegged his age to be midtwenties. "How'd it happen?"

His turn to look embarrassed. "I got backed over by a Humvee."

I wasn't quite sure what to say to that and fell back on an old holiday favorite. "Well, at least you get to spend Christmas with your family."

He nodded again and looked at the riptide effect that the doors, which continued to open and slide shut, were having on the snow. "My father, he's the only one left — no brothers and sisters. I'm it." He glanced back up at me. "He was a jarhead, Third Division — Vietnam like you, Con Thien in '67."

I leafed through my military history and came up with the combat base that was only three kilometers from North Vietnam. The site of numerous battles, it was known to most Marines as "The Meat Grinder." "Gung ho."

"Yeah, he's pretty proud of that."

"Well, he must be glad to have you home."

His response held little enthusiasm. "Yeah." Another couple emerged, this time pausing to place a box with an electronic robot in the chaplain's hand. "Thank you both and have a Merry Christmas." He watched them half walk, half slip to their vehicle and then placed the toy in the half-full bin. "You have family inside?"

"My daughter."

He looked beyond the large maroon

metal–framed doors. "The redhead?"

"Yep."

"She waved and knew my rank."

"She would."

He glanced at me again, just to make sure I knew that there was no disrespect intended. "If you don't mind me saying so, sir — she's hot." I raised an eyebrow, and he shrugged a response. "Hey, I said I was a chaplain, not a eunuch."

I laughed. "She's in the process of trying to cajole me out of my bad holiday mood."

"Hey, it could be worse; you could be like my father and be in a bad mood year-round. I think it's hard for him; I mean, all he does is sit around the house and read the newspaper."

I wasn't quite sure what to say to that either, so I just stood there.

After a few swishes of the door, which produced one Barbie princess, he spoke again. "He's not a bad guy, my old man, but I don't think he understood me joining the Navy and certainly not me joining the clergy." He paused again. "He was a career Marine, and he keeps asking me about medals. You know, why it is that I don't have any."

I glanced down at the service bars and on his chest, the Purple Heart visible just under the sling.

"He says those don't count." He re-arranged the injured arm and placed the other hand in his pants pocket. "I get the feeling that he thinks I'm some kind of . . . I don't know."

I thought about how the Army and the Marines had lost a hundred chaplains between them during WWII — the third highest mortality rate behind the infantry and Army Air Corps — and how, on the USAT *Dorchester* in 1943, four chaplains had given their life jackets, and in so doing, their lives, for others.

"I'm sure he's very proud of you." I paused a moment. "When I was in Vietnam, I remember thinking how I was glad that I wasn't the guy without a weapon."

He smiled at me, and, as he accepted a *Spirit* DVD for the cause, I could hear that there seemed to be some sort of hubbub going on at the center of the store — prob-ably a fight over the latest Gameboy.

"It takes a lot of guts to be in the thick of it on the front lines with nothing to take cover behind other than your convictions."

The young ensign nodded and looked at his highly polished shoes as the doors opened and shut two more times.

I glanced back at him and was beginning

to think I'd overstepped when he spoke again. "Hey, I just sometimes wish that something had happened to me over there other than getting backed over by a truck. You know, something that I could be proud of when I talk to the old man."

I looked over his head and could clearly see that something was happening inside the store as employees seemed to be converging and customers appeared to be moving away, some of them exiting very quickly and rushing by us into the parking lot without a thought of a toy for a tot. "Well, careful what you wish for. I'm betting you'll be going back."

"No, I'm getting stationed stateside: Naval Base Point Loma, California." He shrugged again. "I guess they decided I wasn't battlefield material." He looked sad at the idea. "At least it'll be warmer."

The doors opened again, and this time I could hear people screaming and yelling. The young officer took a step toward the store.

"Something going on in there?"

I leaned sideways and could see a tall man push someone in a blue and yellow Best Buy vest and start toward us with something under his jacket. "I'm not sure."

The employee who had been shoved

153

grabbed the man by the shoulder, but the large guy turned and made a quick, jerking move with his free hand and the employee hugged his arm and fell on the floor.

The big fellow took off at a dead run toward us, but as I started to move around Burch, he sidestepped directly in front of me. "What's going . . ."

The large man, still holding something under his parka, charged through the sliding glass door into us.

Burch was stormed over and fell backward into one of the concrete parking impediments, almost taking me with him, but I was lucky enough to latch onto the guy's arm. I spun him around into the steel-reinforced glass beside the door, and his nose made the sound of a saltine cracker being neatly snapped in two. The laptop computer he'd been holding fell from his coat, along with the nylon-handled knife he'd had in the other hand.

He stood there for the briefest of moments and then took two and a half staggering steps before falling backward onto the hood of the Jeep, the irises rolling back in his head. I kicked the knife toward the ensign, who was working himself up onto his hand and knees.

Turning and grabbing the thief by the coat

front, I lifted him a little further onto the hood of the Wrangler, pulled the handcuffs from my belt, and secured one of his wrists to the Jeep's side-view mirror.

I reached down and helped Burch to his feet, scooped up the wicked-looking blade, and placed it in the sling hand. "Hey, that was something."

He crooked his neck and looked up at me, stretching his eyelids as he massaged his recovering shoulder and stared at the knife in his hand. "What?"

People spilled from the store now, employees and customers alike, attempting to get a look at what had happened. I raised my voice to be heard over the general noise: "The way you took that guy out — that was something."

Pulling my cuff keys from my belt, I slipped them into the breast pocket of his jacket. "The Billings PD should be here in about five minutes give or take."

I stooped again, this time picking up the damaged computer and handing it to the store manager with the nametag that read DALE. "Did you see that? Boy howdy, that was something else."

Dale looked at the chaplain, who was still shaking his head and looking a little confused. "He did that?"

"Single-handedly." I glanced at the young man's sling and resisted making further comment.

It was about then that I felt someone grab my arm, crowding in close. "Daddy, you are not going to believe what just happened. This guy was stealing a laptop and then security confronted him and the guy started yelling and pulled out this knife . . ." Cady looked past me to the man lying on the hood of the Jeep, still unconscious. "Oh, wow."

I reached down and took her shopping bag, pulled Cady's receipt out, and tore the end off. I plucked the pen from my shirt, scribbled a number down on the paper, and handed it to the manager. "Call Chris Rubich from the *Gazette* right now and you can get this in tomorrow's paper; it's good advertising and you've got a heck of a human interest story here."

He nodded his way back into the store with the number in his hand and the laptop under his arm. I propelled my daughter past the gathering crowd but paused long enough to catch the eye of the chaplain, still trying to gather his wits. "Heck of a job — just a heck of a job."

I steered Cady past the Wrangler into the parking lot through the swirling snow and toward my three-quarter-ton as she whispered, "Did you have anything to do with that?"

"No."

"Daddy?"

"No, I didn't." I loaded her in, started the engine, and began backing out as a Billings City Police car with siren trumpeting and light bar twinkling sledded across four lanes of opposing traffic and beelined for the Best Buy entrance.

As I waited, Cady leaned down and pulled out an interactive child's reader from one of her shopping bags. "Damn it, I meant to put this in that ensign's toy bin but you rushed us out of there so fast." She unhooked her seat belt. "I'll be right back."

"I don't think that's such a great idea."

She climbed out the passenger-side door. "I won't be long, Dad. Honest Injun." She grinned at me and tossed her head, strawberry blond hair in full sway.

I sighed and watched in the rearview mirror as she ran, careful to avoid the Billings patrolmen as they loaded the would-be thief into the back of their cruiser. She paused and spoke to Burch, put the reader in the TOYS FOR TOTS box, and laughed.

Dog whined, and I reached back and petted him. "It's all right. She'll be here in a minute."

Three delayed slaps of the windshield wipers and she'd returned.

She climbed in, shut the door behind her, and rehooked the belt as I slipped the truck into gear and pulled into the light traffic of King Avenue. There were about two inches on the road, and it felt like we were driving on a thick bed of quilt batting. Cady seemed preoccupied with the falling snow darting through the headlights like neon guppies, but I had to admit that my mood had improved.

We were through the underpass and rolling quietly onto the blanketed surface of I-90 when, with a knowing smile, Cady reached up and clicked my Peerless, stainless steel handcuffs onto the rearview mirror.

# DIVORCE HORSE

It was Memorial Day weekend, and I was having dinner with Henry and Cady at the Busy Bee Café. Still recovering from my experiences chasing after escaped convicts in the Bighorn Mountains, I fingered the oversize ring on my thumb and watched the turquoise wolves chase the coral ones on the silver band; then I plucked it off and stuffed it in my shirt pocket under my badge.

I'd been sheriffing solo since Vic had flown back to Philadelphia for the long Memorial Day weekend to help her mother with the arrangements for Cady and her brother Michael's upcoming wedding. It was complicated. Boy howdy.

Generally, Cady and Vic just shared a cup of coffee in the Denver airport as they traded time zones during their assorted holiday layovers, but on this stint Cady had driven Vic to the airport in Billings. They'd had more time to talk and had engaged in what I'd feared could be a wide-ranging conversation.

Cady sat still. "Vic looks really good."

I sipped my iced tea and joined Henry in studying Clear Creek's fast-flowing water as it riffled by the café in a torrent of melt from the Bighorns. "Yep."

The Greatest Legal Mind of Our Time leaned in with a few strands of strawberry blond hair slipping in front of her face, reminding me so much of her mother. "She bought a house?"

"Yep."

"So she's sticking around."

I turned my head, aware that Henry wasn't the only one occupied with fishing, and studied my daughter. "I didn't know that she had been talking about going anywhere."

She brushed away my remark with a fan of her fingers. "I just wasn't sure if she'd stick."

I considered the statement. It was true; the high plains were a place of transition — people came, people went, few stayed. Economics had a lot to do with it, but so did the loneliness of the topography. It was as if the land hollowed out spaces in people until they treated each other with that same distance — some never came to a truce with that within themselves. Vic had threatened to run off with the Feds and a number of other agencies, and had even thought about Philadelphia again, but those threats seemed to come less and less often. "I think she likes it here."

"I think she likes parts of it." Cady took a sip of her diet soda, part of her continuing effort to fit into a size 2 by the July wedding. "How old is she again?"

Reaching for my glass, I almost tipped it over but caught it in the last instant. "We've . . . never discussed that."

She nudged the Cheyenne Nation with her shoulder. "How old is she, Bear?"

He shrugged. "I have found in most relationships with women it is best to remember their birthdays but forget their age."

"Look who I'm asking." She rolled her eyes and redirected them, looking into the golden light reflecting off the buildings on the east side of Main Street. The stores were staying open just a little longer than the usual five p.m. in the hopes of plying the tourist trade that the American Indian Days Parade and Powwow had engendered. Most of the crowd had adjourned to the county fairgrounds, but the barely beating heart of

161

commerce sprang eternal.

I glanced at Henry, who continued watching the water.

She leveled her cool, gray eyes on my face. "So, what's going on with you two?"

Tipping my hat back, I turned to give her a stare. "That would be in the none-of-your-business file."

She slid down in her chair and twisted the hair that had escaped her ponytail around her index finger. "How come I can't ask you about your personal life, but you can ask me about mine?"

The Cheyenne Nation grunted but said nothing, avoiding the table's verbal minefield.

I nudged my glass and glanced around to make sure that no one else was within ear reach, but the only other patrons on that remarkably clear, warm, and velvety early evening were a threesome of cowboys at a table by the front door, and Dorothy, the owner and proprietor, who was busily putting our dinners together. "I have never asked you about your personal life, ever."

She thought about it and then grinned. "I kind of volunteer it, don't I?"

Henry smiled. I didn't say anything.

"Sometimes too much?" She fingered her napkin, and I noticed that her nails were blush pink and not their usual dark red. She must be practicing bridal etiquette.

From the radio behind the counter, Hank Williams was crooning "You're Gonna Change (Or I'm Gonna Leave)." I thought maybe I should soften my response. "It's normal — women ask about relationships, but men hardly ever do."

She slipped on the smile she always did when she didn't particularly believe what I was saying — I had gotten that smile since she was six. "Never?"

I glanced at the Bear and watched as he turned to Cady, his voice rumbling in his chest. "Hardly ever."

"I don't believe that."

I shrugged and sipped mine as Dorothy arrived with two deluxe chicken-fried-steak sandwiches piled high with fries, and another plate with a small mound of cottage cheese and a couple of cherry tomatoes. I asked, purely for form's sake, "The usual?"

She placed the plates in front of us and raised an eyebrow. "Which one?"

I pointed at the marginal board of fare on Cady's plate. "Not that."

Dorothy smirked. "I've named that Chef's Choice." She put a bottle of no-fat, low-calorie balsamic vinaigrette in front of Cady and glanced around. "How are the sheriff's

163

department, Indian scout, and learned counsel tonight?"

"Hopefully slow." I checked my pocket watch. "Especially since — with the exception of Ruby at the office and Saizarbitoria down at the fairgrounds — I gave the rest of the staff the night off." I returned the watch to my pocket and unrolled my napkin, depositing the flatware by my plate, not because I needed it but because I thought I'd better put the napkin on my lap. "And Ruby's off in three minutes."

Dorothy's attention was drawn back to Cady, who had reached for the salad dressing. "How are you, sweet pea?"

"I'm good." She rearranged the tomatoes. "Business finally slowing down?"

Dorothy sat on a stool adjacent to the counter and rubbed her ankle. "Yeah, finally. It was crazy all day, especially during the parade. This is the first chance I've had to sit down. I think everybody's out at the Powwow now." She reached over and tugged on the Bear's hair, and I tried to remember if I'd ever seen anybody do that except her. "Damned Indians. I suppose people would just as soon eat fry bread and cotton candy." She glanced at me and then back to Cady. "Your father lure you away from that young man of yours?"

"Just till I'm sure he's feeling better after his mountain adventure." My daughter's eyes held on me for a moment, and I could see the worry there. "And besides, I figured I'd stick around a little while and see if I could get some preliminary wedding work done. You know I want you to make the cake, right?"

"Planning on it. I'm consulting with Vic's uncle Alphonse next week about the recipe." She let go of her leg and stood up. "You're getting married up on the Rez, right?"

I felt a private little sorrow overtake me about the eventuality of losing her but continued eating.

"Yeah, Crazy Head Springs."

"That's a pretty spot. Have you gotten permission?"

Cady nudged the Bear's shoulder. "I've got an *in.*"

Dorothy laughed and kissed the top of Cady's head. "Congratulations, honey."

Cady glowed. "Thanks."

The owner/operator glanced at the three cowboys, whom I recognized as Matt Hartle and two of the wranglers from Paradise Guest Ranch; Matt raised his coffee mug as the others smiled at us.

"I better go refill the Wild Bunch over there." She placed her fists on her hips.

"You folks need anything else?"

Cady volunteered. "I might switch over to coffee, when you get the chance."

Dorothy winked and disappeared.

Cady began nibbling at a forkful of cottage cheese but stopped just long enough to give the Bear and me a warning look. "Don't say it." She caught another curd on the end of her fork and then used it like a baton to get my attention. "I still don't believe that women ask more about personal issues than men. I mean, maybe men hide the question more, but it's there."

Henry said nothing, so I spoke for the two of us. "Okay."

She ate the bit of food. "But the two of you believe it."

I paused with the sandwich only inches from my mouth. From all my years in law enforcement I knew that the only thing that happened more than not getting to eat was having your meals interrupted and abandoned. I looked at Henry, and we both turned and answered her in unison. "Yep."

Buck Owens swung into "Before You Go," and Cady sang along in her fine voice in a pretty good imitation; I was starting to think we had a soundtrack on our hands, but then she suddenly stopped, looked at the two of us, and I knew we were in trouble. "How

166

about a bet, a sporting wager?" She continued before I could say no. "For every woman who asks either one of us about our relationships or every man who doesn't, you two get a point. For every woman who doesn't ask us about our relationships or every man that does, I get a point."

Knowing my daughter's level of competition in all things, I knew this was a bad idea and said so.

She wheedled. "Come on, Daddy. It'll be fun."

Henry leaned over and gave her the horse-eye, up close and personal. "One to nothing then."

Cady glanced at Dorothy pouring her a cup of coffee behind the counter, and then back to the Bear. "We haven't started yet."

I was shaking my head when the walkie-talkie on my hip chattered to life.

Static. "Unit one, this is base."

I slumped in my seat, dropped my sandwich in dramatic fashion, and sat there for a moment.

Static. "Walt?"

My daughter, who could never resist pushing buttons, plucked the device from my duty belt and keyed the mic. "Yo."

Static. "Cady?"

I took the radio from her. "It's after five

167

— go home."

Static. "Tommy Jefferson says one of his horses has been stolen out at the rodeo grounds."

I gazed at my half-eaten meal and sighed. "Not the divorce horse again?"

Static. "Of course."

The much-storied case of the divorce horse was the kind of situation familiar to most rural sheriffs, one of those disputes you ended up getting involved in even though it had nothing much to do with law enforcement. Tommy Jefferson and his ex-wife Lisa Andrews were Cady's age. He was a New Grass from Crow Agency, Montana, who had lived with an aunt in Durant so that he could go to our high school and who had subsequently developed into a world-class Indian horse relay rider. She was a blond whirlwind of a barrel racer. Their romance had been epic; seven years later, their divorce was a long and familiar story.

Tommy had had a bad habit of loitering at equine sales and was already a frustrated horse trader before their marriage, but it only got worse as he and Lisa joined incomes and as he intensified his use of diet pills in an attempt to keep his racing weight down and his energy level up. It had gotten so bad that Lisa began to think that Tommy was more addicted to horses and amphetamines than to her.

When he brought home a vicious, Roman-nosed, cloudy-eyed little sorrel the color of store-bought whiskey that had a propensity to wander and bite and that took all his time, effort, and attention, Lisa had had enough, and their separation and divorce became a pitched battle. The train wreck that was Tommy and Lisa's lives was played out in every under-the-breath conversation in the county and on the Rez.

My part in the saga had started when Tommy, who had returned to the Rez and to methamphetamines big-time, decided to call the sheriff's office in order to get Lisa to answer his calls. It seemed logical to his chemically addled, emotionally distressed mind that since she was living in Absaroka County, it was my duty to ask her to answer her phone. As a rural sheriff, there are times when the law enforcement side of the job has nothing to do with the right-thing-to-do side of the job.

So, I'd dutifully made the trip down to Powder Junction where they had shared a house, only to discover Lisa, clad in a bikini bottom, a T-shirt, and a potato-chip cowboy hat, sunbathing in her yard. I asked her if she would please answer the phone, because Tommy had been trying to get in touch with her for days.

She took a sip from a can of beer beside her towel and said, "Had it disconnected."

"Do you mind if I ask why?"

"He was calling here twenty times a day, and I couldn't take it anymore." She adjusted the straw hat and sighed. "You know he's still using, right?"

"Um, it's becoming apparent to me." I stood there on the other side of the chain-link fence that separated her yard from the sidewalk. "Well, he'd like you to call him."

Lisa put the can down. "No thanks. I jumped that crazy horse, Sheriff — and I have no intentions of getting back on." She squirted more suntan lotion out of the bottle and began applying it to her arms. "Anyway, I yanked the cord out of the wall."

Then she'd served him papers, and that's when things really got weird.

Tommy began calling me, the county clerk, and Verne Selby, who had been appointed judge in the case, about all kinds of strange things, insinuating that this was obviously a matter of racial discrimination. Anti-Indian bias had led to the current impasse between him and Lisa.

When I stopped taking his calls, he resorted to the fax machine. I would come in mornings to find thirty- and forty-page letters from Tommy, most of them incoherent but each one ending with the request that the communication be dated, stamped, and placed in the official record. Of all the faxed letters, the one that leaps to mind as the strangest was a four-pager instructing the clerk, judge, and me on what it was we should bring to Thanksgiving dinner up on the Rez — how I should bring pie, but not rhubarb since his aunt Carol usually had that covered. Like we were all family.

A standard divorce with a file over fourteen inches thick.

Vic had measured.

"Divorce Horse."

Vic had coined the term.

I keyed the mic again. "Well, then nobody stole it — nobody in their right mind would steal that horse." I looked at the food on my plate, questioning the choice of giving the majority of my deputies the night off. "Isn't Saizarbitoria out there?"

Static. "He's not answering, but that could just be because of the crowd noise."

"I'm on my way."

Static. "Roger that."

I keyed the mic one last time. "Ruby, go home."

Cady worked a little faster on her cottage cheese. "My Tommy Jefferson?"

Cady and he had dated and even went to a junior prom together, but this was nothing unique — my daughter had cut a wide swath in the male populace of Durant High School. "Yep."

Henry chewed quickly as well. "Wow, a case."

I nodded and, thinking about all those phone calls, faxes, and accusations, I absently reached up to rub the top of my ear, which was the locale of persistent frostbite.

Cady swiped at my hand. "Stop that." She studied me. "You don't seem overly enthusiastic."

The assorted injuries I'd sustained on the mountain continued to release a collective groan. "I'm not."

Dorothy arrived with Cady's cup of coffee, and I noticed it had been repoured into a to-go cup. "You know she's back in town, right?"

I glanced up at the chief cook, bottle washer, waitress, and fount of all things social. "Who?"

"Lisa. She was in here yesterday and said she'd rented one of those apartments over by Clear Creek."

I thought about it. "Well, I'm pretty sure it's over between her and Tommy."

Dorothy shrugged and headed back to the counter as Cady wiggled in her chair like she had when she was a kid. "How 'bout I be the lead investigator on this one?"

I stared at her. "You're kidding, right?"

"Nope." She took the last bite of cottage cheese and swallowed, her eyes glittering with anticipation. "How hard can it be?"

The weekend had been blessed with three memorable spring evenings where you could smell the grass in the pastureland, and the sagebrush and cottonwoods that had been holding their breath since October gasped back to life. The cool of the evening was just starting to creep down from the mountains, but it was still T-shirt weather, if long-sleeve T-shirt weather.

We argued as we climbed into the Bullet. "*How's your dog* does not constitute a relationship question."

She ruffled the beast's ears as he laid his head on the center console and sniffed the Styrofoam containers Cady had set at her feet. "It's a relationship; it may not be your only relationship, but it's a relationship."

I lodged the to-go iced tea and Cady's coffee into the holder on the dash, fired up the motor, and pulled the three-quarter-ton down onto the vacant street to follow the Cheyenne Nation's '59 Baltic blue Thunderbird convertible, Lola. "You're cheating already."

"Look, the other two cowboys didn't ask, so it's two to one. I wouldn't complain if I were you." She pulled her coffee from the holder. "Hey, I didn't throw you for a loop with all that wedding talk back there, did I?"

"Do I get a point from this conversation?"

"No."

Heading toward the fairgrounds at the north edge of town, we had driven only a short distance before my truck radio crackled.

Static. "Boss, it's unit two."

Cady, always quicker to the draw, grabbed the mic from my dash. "Unit two, this is unit one. How's the Powwow?"

Static. "Hi, Cady. The natives are restless; at least one of them is."

She keyed the mic. "Did somebody really steal the divorce horse, or was Tommy just high and forgot where he put it?"

Static. "No, he seems pretty straight to me, and the horse is missing."

"We're on our way."

Static. "Roger that."

I glanced at her. "Three to one."

Cars and trucks were parked on the side of the road for a quarter of a mile to avoid the one dollar fee the Rotary collected like they were the Cosa Nostra. A thickset cowboy ambled up to my window.

"Chip."

"Walt." He looked past me and smiled at my daughter, who was making a display with her engagement ring. "Hey, Cady." He returned his attention to me and the smile faded as he stuck a palm out. "Gimme two dollars."

"I'm on a call."

He repeated. "Gimme two dollars."

"It's official."

"Gimme two dollars."

"The sign says a dollar."

Chip looked at the Bear, arrowing for the VIP parking area by the grandstands, and then back at me. "Henry said you'd pay." He took the money and smiled at Cady. "Nice rock. I heard you were getting married?"

She fluttered her eyelashes at him, and it seemed to me she'd dated him at one point, too. "I am."

"Congratulations."

As we pulled in beside Henry, I cried foul. "That was a blatant use of a prop."

She twirled the large diamond on her finger. "What, this little ol' thing?" She opened the door and slid out. "Three–two."

The roar of the crowd intimated that the Indian Relay Races had already begun. The old Native practice involved a single-rider in traditional dress of loincloth and moccasins and three horses, one for each leg of the relay. As the rider leapt from one mount to the other, an unfortunate individual known as a "mugger" had to hold on to the half-wild horse who'd just completed his leg. It made the Professional Rodeo Cowboys Association look like a Harrods afternoon tea.

I followed Henry as he led us through the tunnels that met with the main lateral walkway where we took a left through the throngs toward the paddocks and down a set of steps to the ground level of the grandstand.

Ken Thorpe, another of the Rotary mafia, was leaning against the gate and turned to look at us as we arrived. "Hey, Walt."

"I'm not giving you a dollar."

He looked a little confused. "Okay."

"Tommy Jefferson, New Grass team, had

a horse stolen?"

"Yep, but he's on a spare."

We all crowded at the gate in time to see the riders rounding the near turn, bareback and crouched into the manes of their horses. The men were painted and so were their mounts. One of the beauties of the sport was the pageantry — some of the riders were in full warbonnets, some in shaman headdresses, the riders and their ponies resplendent in team colors, the designs reflecting the lines, spots, handprints, and lightning bolts recorded in the old Indian ledger drawings.

Henry pointed. "That's Tommy in the green."

Sporting the three vertical stripes of the New Grass team, Tommy was charging hard coming up on the last leg of the second part of the relay. It was possible that the young man was simply pacing himself in second place, but it didn't look like it — it looked like the ride of his life.

We watched as they cannoned by, the fine dust of the fairgrounds settling on our hats and shoulders as we all jockeyed to see the riders transfer onto the last horse in the race. It was at this exchange where the majority of wrecks occurred.

The lead rider, a lanky fellow from eastern

Washington's Colville Reservation, always a powerhouse, vaulted from his mount as one of his muggers grabbed that horse's reins while another held the last horse steady. The Spokane Indian misjudged the distance, or maybe the horse made a tiny surge when it felt something leaping onto its back, but the rider managed to grab hold of the mane as the Appaloosa launched skyward before settling into a rocket trajectory past the grandstand, the poor man nearly bouncing off the horse's rump but still hanging on.

The crowd of close to four thousand went crazy, but by that time Tommy Jefferson, New Grass team of the Crow Nation, had leapt from his own mount. His mugger attempted to hold his next horse, but the chestnut was now circling the mugger with Tommy holding on to the mane, one ankle draped over the horse's spine.

The mugger, not knowing what to do, did the only sensible thing and let go. Apparently the only one who knew what he was supposed to be doing was the horse, who reared and blasted down the straightaway with Tommy hanging off the side, as the rest of the field fumbled with their own transfers and fell further behind.

"Oh, no." The Bear, of course, was the first to see the danger.

Tommy was headed straight toward the chutes for the roping and bull-dogging events — massive, metal gates, reinforced with what looked like highway guardrails at the far end of the grandstand. The chestnut, in its attempt to catch up with the Appaloosa, had set a course that would give it the best advantage but would also carry it and its rider next to the metal barrier. We could see that the horse would likely make it, but Tommy, still hanging off him on the side nearest the gate, would not.

Pogo hopping on one foot, the young man was scrambling to get both legs up, but with only about a hundred feet to go, it looked like he had maybe only two hops left.

He wasn't going to make it.

I reached for Cady's hand in an attempt to distract her from what appeared to be Jefferson's imminent death. Her hand was already reaching behind her for mine, and I felt her grip as Tommy postholed one miraculous stamp on the ground and barely slithered past the abutment, his calf grazing the steel fence.

The crowd, which I thought might've already exhausted itself, went ballistic. All four thousand were standing as Tommy rounded the far corner and started gaining on the Colville rider, the rest of the field a far third.

Through the backstretch I could see the Spokane Indian's warbonnet traveling across the infield as if by magic, levitated above the ground and moving across the far rail at close to forty miles an hour. But there was a vengeance that followed him, a Crow centaur who rounded the far corner and blew into the straight like a war lance. You could see Tommy's head tucked into the horse's mane, and maybe it was the whispering of the Indian's voice that carried them along like Crow chain lightning.

The Spokane rider, feeling their breath on the back of his neck, turned to get a glimpse of his pursuer, and when he did, the warbonnet he wore inverted, the eagle feathers tunneling around his face like shaft-shaped blinders. His arm came up to catch it at the crucial moment when they turned the near curve, which caused the Appaloosa to go wide and miss the apex.

Tommy, taking full advantage, veered his pony to the inside, and the two were neck and neck.

From our ground-level viewpoint, it looked as if they were headed straight toward us. As they drew to the corner it appeared as if the Colville rider had the advantage again, but when they rounded the curve nearest us, Tommy had made up the distance on the inside, and they were running as if the two horses were in traces.

They crossed the finish line, no one able to tell which horse had come in first. We'd have to take the judges' word on it.

And the judges' word was that Tommy had lost by a nose.

Henry turned to look at our little group. "It wasn't for lack of trying."

"No." I turned to Ken. "How long till the next race?"

"Oh, it's a good hour. They're doing the fancy dance competition down here in front of the grandstand as soon as they pick up the poop and smooth the track over with the grader."

"Can we cut across to the infield and talk with Tommy?"

"If you give me a dollar." He smiled, then opened the gate and ushered us through.

Saizarbitoria was waiting on the other side. "Did you guys see that?"

I nodded. "I guess he had at least one life left, huh?"

He fell in step as we approached the heated conversation going on over by the announcer's tower, where Tommy was threatening to burn the booth down with flaming arrows if the judges didn't change their call.

Tommy's leg was bleeding, streaking the chartreuse war paint he still wore. "You fuckin' Indians are trying to rob me!"

So much for Native American solidarity.

"Now, Tommy, calm down . . ."

The Colville Agency Indians, far from home and deep in enemy territory, had wisely chosen not to attend the unofficial inquest, so the two camps in contention were Tommy and his muggers — two men almost as big as Henry and me — and the three judges, one of whom, the head judge, happened to be Tommy's uncle.

Richard New Grass glanced over his nephew's shoulder at me and, perhaps more important, at Henry. He nodded at the Bear and turned his attention back to the agitated rider. "It was an electronic finish, Tommy — there's nothing we can do about it. The Colville rider won fair and square, and that's all there is to it." Tipping his trademark black cowboy hat back on his head, Richard turned his patrician face toward me, effectively ignoring his nephew's further protests. "Can I help you, Sheriff?"

"I understand there's been a possible theft? Something about a horse?"

Tommy danced himself between us and

jerked his head in emphasis with every word. "You're damn right there's been a theft — these sons-a-bitches are tryin' to take this race away from me."

Tommy made a dramatic display and turned on the heels of his moccasins, walking between Henry and me toward Cady, who had been standing behind us. "And not only do these damn Indians steal the race, but one of my best rides is gone."

The muggers walked off to wipe down the sweat-marked horses, and I shrugged at Richard and the rest of the judges, who were also leaving the argument, most likely relieved to be rid of the New Grass entourage.

Tommy was walking ahead of us with Cady, and they were both laughing — and I had the feeling I was about to lose a point.

At the outside edge of the infield, they walked towards a trailer attached to a white Dodge half-ton painted with the New Grass green stripes, which stood next to an event tent festooned with the banners of the team's sponsors, most prominently BUCK-ING BUFFALO SUPPLY COMPANY, HARDIN BAIL BONDS, and H-BAR HATS. There were a number of energy drinks and pop in a fifty-gallon cooler, and, after a few plunges into the ice, Tommy finally pulled out three power drinks, one for Cady and one each for Henry and me. "Here, supplied by one of my sponsors."

Cady handed hers back. "Do you have diet?"

"That shit's bad for you." Tommy sighed and, with a shrug, retrieved a bottle of water. "All I got." Then he scooped off his coyote headdress, threw himself into a lawn chair, and looked down at his bloody calf. "Oh, man . . ." He stuck out his tongue in play exhaustion and nodded toward Henry. "Hey, throw me one of those horse bandages, would you?"

Henry did him one better and wrapped the young athlete's leg. "I am sorry you lost."

Tommy shook his head. "Just for show — we won the first heat and Colville came in seventh. We were second in this one, so all we have to do is place higher than they do by less than that in the next heat and we win it all. It's a Calcutta — lots of money riding on this one — could keep us going into next year's competition." He reached over and slapped the Cheyenne Nation's shoulder as Henry taped up Tommy's bandage. "Gotta keep these Indians honest, right, Bear?"

I watched as the Cheyenne Nation stood

but then stooped a little in order to look closely at Tommy's face. "So they tell me."

Tommy, aware he was being inspected, grinned widely. "*Haaho.* New teeth."

Henry nodded. "I thought so."

"Big Horn County jail. The meth ate them out, so they gave me new ones." His hands stroked his arms and then brushed against each other in a demonstration of purification. "I'm clean." His head bobbed, and his eyes darted to Cady. "Damn, you look good, girl. Hey, you know I'm free, right?"

Her face looked sad when she responded. "That's what I heard."

"Yeah, it was a long winter." Jefferson glanced at me, obviously embarrassed about the episodes that had involved the Absaroka County Sheriff's Department and assorted Durant officials. "I still miss her, you know?"

Cady nodded and stood next to his camp chair. "I bet."

Tommy looked up at her. "How about you, are you seeing anybody?"

I got the glance as she showed him the ring. "Yeah, I'm engaged to a guy in Philadelphia — Dad's undersheriff's brother."

He whistled and glanced at me. "Vic?"

I nodded, but Cady answered. "His name is Michael."

He folded his newly clean arms over his lean, horseman's body. "He anything like her?"

She laughed. "No." I watched her study him for a moment and then ask: "I heard about you and Lisa. What happened?"

He ran his fingers through his hair, wet with sweat, the black of it shimmering blue in the half sun. "Oh, I don't know. I guess I got so interested in the horses that she thought I wasn't interested in her anymore." He sighed. "We both got mad and said some things . . . That's when I really got started on the Black Road with the drugs and stuff. I told her I wasn't sure what it was I wanted . . ." He gestured around the dirty infield at the blowing trash. "So here I am, and I guess this is what I wanted." He swung his legs onto the dirt and pushed out of the chair, wincing at the weight on his leg. He glanced at me, possibly unhappy that I was hearing the whole story, then hitched his thumbs into the waistband of his loincloth. "I keep thinking I'll just call, but I made myself a promise that I wouldn't bother her anymore after all that happened."

We stood there for a moment, listening to the drumming and chanting from the fancy dance competition echoing off the grand-

186

stand, no one looking at Tommy, Tommy looking up at the first evening star.

I straightened my hat. "So, what's the story on the div— . . . Um, on the horse?"

His face came back to life. "Well, he's got an adjustable lug on his left shoe, but even so, if we'd had him in this last heat we would've won straight up."

"What happened?"

He shook his head at the injustice. "We had 'em all tied to the back side of the horse trailer over here and when we went to go take 'em to the start, he was missing."

I looked past Saizarbitoria at the two embarrassed muggers. I remembered one of their names. "Markey, you guys look for him in the infield?"

The giant answered, "Yeah, but he's an escape artist, that one. The only one he really liked was Lisa — he'd follow her and nicker and toss his head. Only bit me."

The other giant added, "He can untie knots like a sailor, so I had him clipped. We looked everywhere but he's not here."

Tommy's voice rose from behind me. "Somebody stole him. He's not here, and there's no way he would've crossed the track on his own."

I glanced around the sizable infield — no trees, just dirt and prairie. "No way he

187

could've pulled loose, jumped the railing, and joined in as the horses raced by?"

Jefferson shook his head. "The pickup riders would've gotten him. He was stolen, I tell ya."

I glanced at Henry and watched as he walked between the muggers and rounded the horse trailer. Shrugging, I started after him, noticing my daughter's hands behind her back, three fingers extended on one hand and three on the other: tied.

Ruthless.

I glanced at Saizarbitoria. "You can head back over to the grandstand, Sancho, but turn your radio up so you can hear it."

I joined the Bear between the infield railing and the side of the trailer where the horses were tethered to a piece of rebar steel. Two-year-olds, the horses were skittish and moved away, stamping their hooves and showing us the whites of their eyes.

The Cheyenne Nation reached up and ran a hand over the nearest horse, a dark bay, nut brown with a black mane, ear points and tail, who immediately settled with a sighing rush of air from his distended nostrils; the Bear had magic in his hands, and besides, the animal was probably happy to meet an Indian who wasn't trying to catapult onto his back.

Henry stepped forward and then ducked under the halter leads attached to the bar. Some of the other horses backed away. One tried to rear but was held down by the length of the rope strung through his halter. The Bear mumbled something and they settled as well. Magic, indeed.

At the ends of the leads were metal snaps that could only be manipulated by an opposing thumb, and I didn't see a lot of those around on that side of the trailer.

Henry kneeled and placed his fingertips in the impacted dirt. I felt like I always did whenever I witnessed his intuitive skills. The Bear was a part of everything that went on around him in a way that I could only observe. He had described scenarios to me so clearly that I would have sworn that I'd been there. Crouching behind the trailer and looking at the hitching bar, he sighed. "*If* they had him clipped to the end of the bar — somebody took him."

"Where?"

His dark eyes shifted as he stood, and he walked past the rear of the trailer to run his hand along the inside railing, finally stopping and lifting the top loose. He stared at the ground. "Here, the horse was led through here."

189

I joined him and looked past the dimpled, poached surface of the track at a forgotten gate leading to a fairground building that hadn't been used since they renovated the place back in the eighties. "Across the track and through there — toward the old paddocks."

We stepped through, walked across the track, and opened the top rung of a rail that you'd never have noticed unless you were looking for it. The Bear paused at the end of the walkway that stretched a good hundred yards toward the stalls, the darkness permeated by a rectangular light shining through the windows of the old barn in staccato. "Which do you think will get us first, the black widows or the field mice?"

The place was deserted and looked as if it might collapse at any time, the peeling white paint scaling from the untreated lumber like parchment in abandoned books. "Termites would be my bet."

In the powdery dirt you could see where a horse with an adjustable screw attachment had been walked through. I kneeled this time and studied the boot prints that ran alongside the horse tracks, smallish and worn down on the heels.

"Female, or a very small man."

We were far away from the road and parking lots, which would make it difficult to load an animal into a trailer and whisk it away. That was the beauty of horse stealing, though — you could always ride your stolen property. Of course, that might be difficult to do with a headstrong, half-broke two-year-old that bites. "Did you see how those horses fought the muggers in front of the grandstand?"

"Yes."

"And this horse is the worst of the bunch."

"Yes." He smiled, having the same thought.

We got back to the infield, rounded the trailer, and found Team New Grass and my daughter where we had left them. The muggers were still attending the horses, getting them ready for the next race, while Tommy and Cady sat talking under the tent.

Tommy looked at me, and I had to admit that Trent Burrup, the Big Horn County jail dentist, had done a wonderful job on his teeth. "So, what do I do? Come into the office and fill out some paperwork?"

I pulled up short, took off my hat, and wiped the sweat from my forehead with my shirtsleeve. "Your horse is in the abandoned paddocks across the track in stall number thirty-three."

He looked past my shoulder toward the condemned buildings. "Over there?"

"Yep."

"How the hell did he get over there?"

"No idea."

"How come you didn't bring him back?"

I shook my head. "He wouldn't let me anywhere near him, but we got him blocked off in the stall."

He stood and glanced at the wristwatch on his arm, which looked incongruous against the war paint. "If we hurry we can get him in this next race." He looked down at Cady and took her hand. "I gotta go, but good luck with your marriage." He smiled, the new teeth shining against his dark, paint-streaked face, and held her hands long enough for her to know that he meant what he said next. "There's no way you'll screw it up like I did."

We watched as he walked past the muggers, who were busy currying the next team. They asked if he needed any help, but he shook his head no and lithely jumped over the railing, injured leg notwithstanding.

Markey turned and looked at me. "I'm really sorry about this, Walt. I don't know how it is that he could've gotten out."

"That's okay. We were in the area, and it gave the two of them a chance to catch up."

Cady threw her water bottle in the trash bucket, and we made our way across the infield toward the gate where we'd come in.

Saizarbitoria was standing near the judges' tower and joined us as we walked by. "You find the horse thief?"

"In a way."

Cady volunteered. "The Bear and Dad found the horse over in the old paddocks." She glanced up at Henry and then to me. "He must've wandered off on his own."

"Oh, I wouldn't quite say that."

The Basquo looked at me with a puzzled expression, and I gave him a soft punch in the chest. "I'll tell you about it on Monday."

I'd almost made a clean getaway when he shouted out to my daughter, "Congratulations on the engagement."

Acting as if she was admiring her nail polish, Cady held up four fingers on one hand and three on the other as we walked across the track onto the ramp. Over the loudspeaker, the announcer called all the contestants to the last heat of the World Champion Indian Relay Race.

"Did he just say 'Indian *Really* Race'?" Cady caught my arm as Thorpe shut the gate behind us.

"Just sounds that way with his accent." I kept walking.

"Can we stay for the last go-round, Dad?"

"Why?"

She made a face. "Don't you want to see if Tommy wins?"

We watched as the other teams rode into the area in front of the grandstand, leading their remudas, with Team New Grass suspiciously absent. Cady glanced around and then toward the infield and Tommy's tent. "Do you think he couldn't catch the horse?"

The Cheyenne Nation's voice rumbled as he continued up the ramp. "Possibly."

Cady paused, her hand remaining on the top rail. "He'll miss the race."

The announcer called for Team New Grass to make themselves present at the grandstand or face elimination through forfeiture. I waited a moment more at the gate and then pointed toward the team's muggers and two horses approaching from the infield followed by Tommy, a blond woman, and a frisky two-year-old the color of store-bought whiskey.

I looked past the track and the infield toward the dilapidated stalls on the far end of the fairground. "I guess he just figured out what he really wanted." I held four fingers on one hand and four on the other against my back as I followed the Cheyenne Nation up the ramp.

# THANKSTAKING

"Otis Taylor would've caught that pass."

The Cheyenne Nation eyed me from the other side of the bar and sipped his Armagnac, then glanced up at the tinsel and the vintage ornaments hanging along the beveled mirror at the Red Pony Bar and Grill and Continual Soiree. "I am thinking I queered the deal by putting up the Christmas decorations a day early."

The quiet racket droned on from the 27-inch Sony Trinitron mounted in the corner of the bar as the Chiefs and Broncos locked horns in a lopsided battle for AFC West supremacy — Chiefs 6, Donkeys 27. "You don't think it has something to do with the fact that you have a receiver corps that couldn't catch a cold?"

He watched the TV in a disinterested fashion as another receiver allowed the ball to pass through his gloved fingertips. "It must be cold in Kansas City."

I swiveled on my stool and adjusted the .45 on my right hip. Studying the frost etching the edges of the horizontal windows and the reverse reflection of the red neon Rainier Beer sign glowing in the darkness of the -26 degree high plains evening, I was trying to remember it was still November. "I guess."

KC tried a reverse in the backfield, but either through confusion or nobody wanting the ball, that resulted in a four-yard loss. "No, definitely the Christmas decorations."

I reached down and scratched behind the ears of Dog, aside from Henry, my only Thanksgiving companion. "Are those your grandmother's old ones?"

"Yes." Henry Standing Bear's eyes shifted back to me as he lip-pointed toward the festivities hanging at the back of the bar. "After she died, I never got around to putting up a tree so I decided to use them here."

"They look nice — nostalgic."

He shrugged his massive shoulders, straining the too-small Chiefs jersey with the words YOUR NAME HERE emblazoned across the back. "They make me a little sad, but I put them up anyway."

I sipped my beer and confirmed from his expression that he was going through his usual seasonal melancholy. "Why sad?"

"My grandmother got depressed during the holidays." He reached over and felt the weight of my can, and then automatically slid open the cooler, popped the top of another, and placed it in line behind the first. "Thankstaking was the one she hated the most, though."

I nodded, refusing to snap at the bait of the social argument that we engaged in annually. "How's the turkey coming?"

He studied me again for a second and then pushed off the bar to stir the cranberry sauce and check the brussels sprouts in the oven. Walking over to the back door, he wiped the moisture from the window and looked at the turkey fryer beside the Bullet.

"Why did you park in the back?"

"To keep the drunks from running into my truck." I watched the corners of his mouth pull down and hoped it was in response to the lack of business and not the family holiday depression. "How's the turkey doing?" The Bear could afford a newer, safer cooker — the thing was a festive fire hazard — but he still felt that the five-gallon contraption made the juiciest deep-fried turkey. "How do you know when it's done, other than it blowing up?"

"There will be signs."

I sipped my beer and surrendered the

empty. "Ahh . . ."

He crushed the can in his fist and tossed it into the trash. "Do you know what Columbus wrote about his first encounter with the Bahamian Arawaks who swam out to meet his boat?"

I sighed. "I'm not having this conversation . . ."

His voice took on the phony, authoritative tone of a scholastic filmstrip. " 'They brought us parrots, food, balls of cotton . . . willfully trading everything they owned. They were well built, with good bodies and handsome features, but they do not bear arms, and do not know them, for I showed them a sword, they took it by the edge and cut themselves out of ignorance.' "

". . . Again."

" 'With fifty men we could subjugate them all and make them do whatever we wanted.' "

I nodded toward the game. "Your team is punting."

He ignored it and me, strolled to the end of the bar, and looked out the front window of the converted Sinclair filling station at the darkness of early evening — his thoughts darker still. " 'They would make fine servants.' "

"Umm . . ." I cleared my throat, in hopes

of cutting this conversation short before it became a full-blown tirade. "I like to think of the thanks part of Thanksgiving as giving thanks to the Indians who brought food to the starving pilgrims."

He stayed with his back to me, his voice echoing off the frigid glass. "And in repayment they took everything the Natives had and systematically destroyed them and their way of life?" He turned, and his strong features reminded me of the buffalo nickel. "Ten million Natives lived in what is now the United States when the white man began arriving, and a hundred years later there were less than one million."

I shook my head and stared at him. "Henry, to be honest, I don't know why we do the things we do to each other, or ever have historically. I just know that for me the holidays are for family, friends, and that tiny bit of grace we can afford each other." I raised my beer. "Happy Thanksgiving."

He ignored me. After a few minutes a set of headlights swung into the parking lot, and he returned to the other side of the bar and raised his own brandy glass, but still didn't touch mine. "Thankstaking."

I glanced back at the window where the headlights switched off along with the engine. I reached down and ran my hand across Dog's broad head just so he'd know I wasn't talking about him. "Whoever this is, I hope they've got a more positive seasonal spirit than current company."

Silently we watched the football game, and it seemed to take an awfully long time for whoever it was to come in. Finally, a bearded young man in stained, frayed Carhartt overalls and a coat to match entered the bar and stood at the door. He stared at Dog and me.

"Don't worry, he's friendly." Almost on cue, the beast began emitting one of his low-frequency, idling-motorboat growls. I reached down and pulled his ear. "Knock it off."

He obeyed, but continued to watch the man as he moved to the far end of the bar and sat on one of the stools. He loosened his coat and tipped his ball cap, which bore a welding supply company logo on it, back on his head. Blond hair fell around his red-bearded face. "Can I get a Rainier?"

Henry nodded, fished another can from the cooler, and sat it in front of him. "Tab?"

The guy responded by pulling his keys and some coins from his pocket and scattered them onto the surface of the bar without a word. Henry scooped up the collection of change, returning a dime and a nickel, and then walked back to his vantage point in front of me for a few seconds before continuing toward the back door to check dinner again.

I let Carhartt settle in and get comfortable before reporting on the game, just in case he was interested. "Broncos, by three touchdowns."

He looked at me questioningly.

I shrugged toward the TV. "Football." He unzipped and uncovered a bit more but didn't seem interested in the game. "Passing through?"

He nodded. "Back to Colorado."

"Bakkan?"

He stared at me. "What?"

"The oil fields up in North Dakota."

"Yeah." He sipped his beer. "How did you know?"

"We get a lot of people traveling through, going to or from jobs." I waited another moment and then asked, "You working?"

"Um, yeah." His eyes darted around. "Was."

I nodded and watched as the Bear opened the back door and stepped outside, evidently to check on signs more closely.

The welder stared at the surface of the battered counter, then glanced up at me with his jaw clinched. He shot a look around the bar, almost as if he were casing the joint.

There was something going on with him, and all the alarms were going off in my head. I closed the distance between the bar and me, effectively blocking his view of the clip-holstered .45 attached to my far hip. "Home for the holidays?"

"Um, yeah." He took another gulp of beer and then stood. "Excuse me."

As he headed for the toilets, I swiveled, keeping my sidearm out of sight. Dog growled as he went by, but I nudged him with my boot as Carhartt disappeared.

I thought about how the man had been behaving, then slipped the Colt from my holster and placed it in my lap with my hat over the top. I sat there wondering if I was overreacting when Henry returned, rubbing the cold from his shoulders and looking pointedly at where the welder had been sitting.

"Bathroom."

He came back over and placed his hands on the shelf under the bar, where I knew from experience an Ithaca 10-gauge double-barreled shotgun resided.

I uncovered my sidearm just to show him I was having the same premonition. "Signs?"

He studied the bathroom door over my right shoulder. "The truck plates are from

202

Nevada. It is possible that it is just that it is simply registered there, but he seems edgy."

I covered my .45 again and sighed. "You want me to go outside and run the plates?"

"There is also a woman in the truck and a very small child, both asleep."

I felt some of the coolness drain from my face, and the stillness of my hands slackened. "Not the usual MO for a robber, is it?"

"No."

"You think we're getting scary in our old age — losing our faith in humanity?"

He glanced over my shoulder again. "I would be inclined to agree with you if he were not standing behind you holding a pistol on us right now."

Dog was growling again, but this time I didn't silence him; instead, I braced a boot against the bar and slowly swiveled to my left until I could see him standing there on the small platform about twenty feet away, his arm extended and a 9mm semiautomatic aimed at me.

"I need money."

It's strange, the things that go through your head when you've got a gun pointed at you. I suppose most people get a little nervous, but I've had so many pointed at me in my career that the thrill is gone —

203

instead, the training kicks in and you start thinking in a tactical sense, taking into consideration the distance, exactly where your assailant is pointing his weapon, exactly what kind of weapon, how fast you can draw yours, and how quickly your two backups are going to react.

By all accounts, the young man was dead and he didn't even know it.

"I need money."

Dog continued to growl, and I smiled. "I think we got that."

"I don't normally do this kind of thing . . . I've got a wife and kid. I mean, this is not who I am. I lost my job and I need to get back to Elko —"

"I thought it was Colorado?"

"Shut up." He shook the gun at me in an attempt to stop my words. "I need money for gas . . . and food."

Maybe it was his sixth sense, or a sign that I'd given the Bear, but he placed a hand on my shoulder just as the thought of introducing my own weapon made a drive-by in my mind.

His voice was easy and conversational. "What kind of gun is that?"

The robber's eyes shifted from me, to Dog, and then back to Henry. "What?"

I could see that both of the Cheyenne

Nation's hands were spread across the bar like powerful spiders. "The semiautomatic you're holding — what kind is it?"

He actually kicked it sideways in an attempt to read the name of the manufacturer on the slide action. "I don't know, it's a . . . I don't know." He pointed it back at us. "Look, I need money."

"And I need a gun." I joined the welder in looking at the Bear as he turned and hit the NO SALE button on the old brass register, the cash drawer flying open like a jutting jaw. Henry reached in and pulled out a wad of twenties and fifties, quickly counting them out on the surface of the bar without taking his eyes off the man. "Four hundred and seventy dollars, and I can throw in the eighty-five cents for the beer."

"I can't sell you my gun."

"Why not?"

It took him a while to come up with a reason. "I'm kind of using it right now."

I could imagine the thin-as-a-paper-cut smile that Henry Standing Bear was smiling behind me as he spoke. "I am proposing an alternative."

He reassessed his aim toward the Bear. "How 'bout I just keep my gun and take all your money?"

The voice that answered was resigned and

just a little sad. "That is not what will happen, and all the other options will end badly for you." He nudged my shoulder and gestured toward the gunman and, more specifically, the gun. "Does that seem like a fair offer?"

My turn to growl. "I think you're overpaying."

He leaned forward on the bar, his large arms folded yet relaxed. "I do not have much time for gift gathering this season, so we will consider it as payment for your services as a personal shopper."

The gunman paused and then gestured with the pistol. "Give me the money first."

I glanced at the Bear, but he didn't look at me, his voice remaining steady. "All right."

I watched as he disappeared, crossing behind me and coming out from behind the bar near the back door. He continued toward the young man, stepped between the two of us, and then held the money out to him. The Bear knew full well that I'd taken advantage of his standing in front of me to draw my Colt and by now had it pointed straight at the man, one of the oldest tricks in the book, but instead of stepping aside, he remained there between us, protecting the gunman.

The welder reached for the cash, but Henry drew it back, just a little. "There is one last thing, though."

The young man cocked his head and kept the 9mm on the Cheyenne Nation. "Yeah?"

"We are about to eat, and there is too much food; I will purchase the gun from you on the condition that you bring your wife and child in here and join us for dinner before continuing your journey."

I watched the welder's eyes and finally saw them soften, almost as if he'd forgotten the gun in his hand. There was a long pause, the muted noise from the TV the only sound. The young man sighed deeply, and his entire body relaxed a little. "We don't want to be a bother."

Henry held the money out. "It is not a bother . . . It is a deal."

This time without hesitation, the gunman lowered the hammer on the semiautomatic and handed it to the Bear. Henry made him take the money, including the pocket change. "Go get your family."

I quietly slipped the .45 back into its holster and watched as the young man left, tucking the wad of cash into his Carhartts as the door swung closed behind him. Henry walked back behind the bar to stir the cranberry sauce and then returned to the back door to check the brussels sprouts and give the turkey one last look.

"How do you know he'll come back?"

He stood there, looking out the door. "Signs."

After a moment he crossed behind the bar again and rested the pistol by the cash register. He stood there for a moment with his back to me and then turned and placed the gunman's keys between us.

He said nothing more, so I lifted my Rainier and watched as he picked up the stemmed glass of Armagnac. He held it out in a mutual toast, and as I touched the aluminum to the glass, I provided the words he could not bring himself to say. "Happy Thanksgiving, Henry."

# MESSENGER

It was one of those late summer days that sometimes showed up in early October after a killing frost — warm, dry, and hazy; Indian summer. The term is over two hundred years old, coined in 1778 by the French American writer J. Hector St. John de Crèvecoeur to describe the warm calm before the winter storm.

Boy howdy.

If one of these miraculous days happened to appear on an autumn Saturday in north central Wyoming, Henry and I would head up into the Bighorn Mountains in pursuit of rainbow, brown, brook, and cutthroat trout. One late afternoon, we were returning from one of those trips with a cooler of fish. By that time in the season, the aspens had turned a shimmering gold in counterpoint to the dense verdant green of the conifers. The made-for-me VistaVision effect was ruined by only one thing: due to the rough road leading into and out of one of our favorite spots along Baby Wagon Creek, relatively unknown to the greater fishing population, I was forced to accompany the Bear in his truck, Rezdawg, a vehicle I hated beyond all others.

Making the environs more decorative, however, was Vic, who had decided to join us on the spur of the moment. She was seated between Henry and me, and I glanced at her, dressed in tight jeans, hiking boots, and a hooded Philadelphia Flyers sweatshirt. The buds of her iPod were in her ears, her eyes were closed, and she was ignoring everything, including me.

We'd just rounded a corner when Rezdawg's wrinkled right fender collided with one of the aspens, which scraped along the door and knocked into my elbow. It might've collided with the passenger side mirror if there had been one, but we'd knocked that off a mile back. The trunk was a little bit bigger in circumference than a Major League Baseball bat.

"Ouch."

Diving between two more trees before heaving the vintage 4×4 over a rock outcropping on top of a small ridge and then sliding down the other side, the Bear sawed at the wheel and looked at me rubbing my elbow. "Are you okay?"

I opened the glove compartment, which contained a pair of work gloves, a box of fuses, an old radiator cap, a seventeen-year-old vehicle registration, and a large mouse nest, but not one Band-Aid. "Scarred for life." I glanced back at him, unsure of what to make of the attention, but then focused on Vic's head instead, bobbing along with the music playing so loudly we could hear it, too. "I don't think she's concerned for my welfare."

"Do you think she is upset about not catching any fish?"

"If she was, she should've tied a fly on the end of her line and put it in the water — that's where I usually catch fish." I reset the handheld radio that kept trying to ride up under my rump and placed it back between Vic and me. "Are you sure this is the way we came in?"

He shot me a look, the corners of his mouth pulled down like guidelines on an outfitter's wall tent. "Shortcut."

"Uh-huh."

The handheld radio chattered briefly, but it had been doing that all day; set on scan, it was picking up the signals from the sheriff's department, the highway patrol, the forest service, and the wardens from game and fish. I picked the thing up and toyed with the squelch in an attempt to get better reception, but it didn't seem to do any good. "Wardens must be busy . . ."

The Cheyenne Nation nodded. "Hunting season and the last of the tourists."

I pointed toward the road, or the lack thereof. "If you'd pay more attention to where we're going, you might save some of these trees." He ignored me, and I continued to fiddle with the knobs on the police radio, the only concession I made to my full-time job while fishing. In my line of work, it's sometimes important for people to get in touch — not too often, but sometimes.

I could feel his eyes on me as he looked past Vic, grooving in her own world. "What?"

He did his best to sound innocent, something he wasn't particularly good at. "What?"

"Why are you behaving strangely?"

He turned back to the road. "Define strangely."

"You keep watching me and asking me if I'm all right."

He didn't turn to look at me this time. "Are you?"

"Yep." I sighed. "You didn't answer my

212

question."

"As a good friend . . ." He sounded annoyed now. "Can I not simply be interested in your general well-being?"

"No, not really." I played with the radio again and thought about what this kind of inordinate attention usually meant. "Have you been talking to Cady?" Newly married, she was pregnant with her first child, but still liked to treat me as if I were one. "What've the two of you been cahooting about now?"

He shook his head. "I know you are in the suspicion business, but your paranoia may be getting the best of you."

"Are you saying you haven't been talking with her?"

"No."

"No what?"

He shook his head solemnly. "No, I did not say that."

"No, you haven't been talking to Cady or no you didn't say that?"

"Exactly."

I shook my head and watched the passing scenery as we bumped along.

After a few moments, he spoke again, just as I knew he would. "I am supposed to broach a subject with you."

"Ahh . . ." This is the way it usually

worked; Cady, sometimes unwilling to ask me questions on more sensitive issues, would ask the Bear to intercede and bring up the subject, floating a topic so she could gauge the response before the real familial debate began. "What's this about?"

"Your granddaughter."

I took a breath, realizing the subject matter was of true import. "Okay."

"She is going to need a name."

I nodded. "Tell my daughter I agree, the child should have a name."

He quickly added, ignoring the humor, "It is a question of *what* name."

I smiled. "We discussed that when she was here for rodeo — she's going to name her Martha."

Henry had been friends with both of us long before we'd gotten married. There was a long pause as the Cheyenne Nation fought the wheel, the road, and possibly me.

I turned and looked at him. "She's not going to name her daughter after her mother?" He shrugged. "We talked about this; we sat there in the bleachers at rodeo and she brought up her mother's name and I seconded it."

"She says you are the one who brought up Martha's name."

"I wasn't."

"She said she mentioned something about the baby's name and that you brought up Martha."

"I just brought her mother's name up casually in conversation, and then she said she was going to name the baby after her."

He shook his head some more. "When you bring Martha's name up in conversation, it is never casual."

We drove in silence, hearing only the music in Vic's ears.

"I might've brought it up un-casually." He continued to say nothing, which spoke volumes. "So, she doesn't want to name the baby after her mother?"

"She is not sure."

"Fine."

"Obviously, it is not."

"I just . . ." My voice sounded a little confrontational even to me, so I changed my tone. "It's just that I'd gotten used to the idea."

"Your idea."

"Evidently." We glanced off another tree, but they were fewer and farther between. "What does she want to name the baby?"

"Lola."

"She wants to name my granddaughter after your car?"

He gestured toward the vehicle in which

we rode. "At least she is not going to name her Rezdawg."

"Lola, really?"

"Yes."

I thought about it. "Where did the name of your car come from?"

"There was a lovely young woman from South Dakota . . ."

"The stripper?"

He smiled a knowing smile. "She was a dancer, yes."

"A stripper; she was a stripper from over in Sturgis that you dated in the seventies."

"She was a very talented performer."

"And you named the car after her."

"Yes."

"I'm not having my granddaughter named after a car named after a stripper." I shook my head. "Lola Moretti. Lola Moretti?"

Vic chimed in for the first time, and I noticed she'd taken the buds from her ears and was cupping them in her hand. "Sounds like a pole dancer to me."

Static. ". . . A couple of lives endangered, and if we don't get any help here pretty soon I'm going to have to do something drastic."

Henry, Vic, and I looked at the handheld radio in my grip — surprised at the interruption.

I punched the button on the mic and

responded. "This is Walt Longmire, sheriff of Absaroka County. Copy?"

Static. ". . . Crazy Woman Canyon, and the situation is pretty serious. We can't get to our vehicles and . . ." The sound drifted off, and I glanced at Henry. ". . . Without backup I'm going to have to use my gun."

I keyed the mic again; it sounded like Chuck Coon, one of the forest service rangers. "Chuck, this is Walt Longmire. Over?"

The Bear mumbled under his breath. "Did you say Chuck? Chuck Coon?"

I nodded and smiled. Coon was actually a very nice guy — he wasn't the kind of ranger who would cite you if your campfire was an inch too close to the trail or your horse was picketed a little too near a water source. Henry, however, had had a few visits with him about the difference between brook trout and brown trout and the number of each species allowed a day, but ever since I had dissuaded a group of motorcyclists traveling from Sturgis from beating Coon to death at West Ten Sleep Campground, the ranger had pretty much decided we were best friends. "Sounds like he's in trouble."

Henry shrugged. "We could go help whoever is trying to kill him."

I thought about the distance between

·e we were now and where the ranger
.. "How long do you think it'll take us to
get there?"

"Not too long."

Looking out the window to avoid Henry's
intermittent gaze as we glanced off another
tree, I folded my arms on my chest. "Lola."

Henry remained resolute. "It is a lovely
name."

Vic shrugged. "She's my niece, and I vote
for Lola. We just better start stocking up on
body glitter."

Passing Muddy Creek forest station, Henry
accelerated into the turn and slowed at the
dirt road marked Crazy Woman Canyon, a
spot in the Bighorn Mountains where a set-
tler family had been decimated, leaving only
the mother who had, reasonably, lost her
mind, the incident made famous in the
Robert Redford film *Jeremiah Johnson.*
"Did Coon say Crazy Woman Canyon or
the campground at Crazy Woman Creek?"

"There is no campground in the canyon,
but there is one at the north fork of the
creek." I braced a hand on the dash and
again reached around for a seat belt, even
though I knew there were none.

My undersheriff looked to our left. "He
must've been confused."

218

Henry hit the gas, the engine wheezed, and we lugged our way up the hill, finally lashing back onto route 16 and flailing the quarter of a mile down the pavement.

Vic pointed past Henry up the small valley. "There — I can see a forest service vehicle with the light bar on."

The Bear spun the wheel, and we flat-tracked our way northwest, sliding to a stop beside a silver Mustang with California plates and a Federal Standard 595 mint-green truck with the driver's-side door hanging open. There was a Porta Potty nearby, on top of which were two people who I gathered were trying to get away from a large sow black bear and her two adolescent cubs milling around the base of the convenience.

As the Cheyenne Nation slid to a stop from a distance of about sixty feet, he rolled the window down, and Vic called out. "Hey, Chuck, looks like there's a line for the john."

I hoisted myself up onto the sill of the passenger-side window and looked over the top of Rezdawg's headache rack as the younger bears, munching on what appeared to be a large amount of popcorn scattered across the ground, glanced at us for a moment before resuming their snuffling around the one-seater. The sow, all six hundred pounds of her, left the snack food and the area around the Porta Potty and ambled two steps our way, grumbling a little and then bouncing up on her hind legs to sniff the air in our direction.

Henry didn't move, his own elbow still hanging from the driver's-side window. "Looks like she is on-the-fight."

Vic glanced through the windshield at the two on the roof and then back to the three bears, raising her voice to be heard. "Hey, Chuck, what were you doing, looking for a Porta Potty that was just right?"

Maintaining his position, but allowing his legs to drop over the side, he adjusted his campaign hat and glanced at the young woman who was with him. "This is Ms. Andrea Napier from Pasadena. She thought it might be fun to feed the bears a bag of caramel corn."

I waved at the young woman. "Hi, Andrea."

She waved back but without much enthusiasm. "Hi."

I ducked my head down and looked at the Cheyenne Nation. "How attached are you to those fish we caught?"

He sighed, relinquishing the idea that trout was going to be the special at the Red Pony Bar and Grill tonight.

Vic and I watched as the Bear nonchalantly opened the door of the truck, slid his chukka boots onto the gravel of the parking lot, and faced the bear. The sow leaned a little forward and huffed at him again but didn't take any further aggressive action. Henry slowly raised a hand and spoke in a calming voice. "Hello, little sister; you should not let your young ones eat such things." He reached into Rezdawg's bed, flipped open the old metal Coleman cooler, covered with stickers, and pulled out the plastic tray containing all the beautiful cleaned fish.

He tossed one of the brookies to the sow, and she immediately dropped onto all fours, landing a paw on the tail of the fish and pulling it apart, devouring it head first. "That is much better for you; you are going into the winter's sleep soon and need to eat healthfully."

The younger bears took notice, but by the time they got to their mother she had already eaten the fish; then all three looked up at the Cheyenne Nation in expectation, Henry slowly creeped forward, calling up to the ranger. "Hey, Chuck, I am not sure if these are brownies or brookies and whether we have sixteen apiece of the one and three of the other; do you want to check them?"

Coon called back, "Ha. Ha."

Henry pulled another trout from the tray and tossed it away from the facility. One of the adolescents ran after it; then he tossed another for the second, and finally another for the sow. Slowly, the Bear led the bears toward Crazy Woman Creek and away from Chuck Coon and Andrea Napier.

After a few moments, I slid back in the window of Rezdawg, climbed out, and held the door open for Vic. We walked around the front of the truck so as not to interrupt Henry's progress with the bears and approached the structure, marveling at the effort it must've taken to get atop the thing. "Jeez, Chuck, how did you get up there?"

He gestured toward the woman, who was clutching the vent stack that protruded from the roof. "She was first, and then she helped me up." He stuck out a pant leg with a shredded cuff and a little blood on the sock and hiking boot. "I barely made it — no pun intended."

I reached up and gestured for Ms. Napier to ease herself off the roof and then lowered her to the ground. She was a handsome thing, outdoorsy and athletic looking with red hair and a slight sunburn, just the kind of woman you might want to be stuck on a roof with, actually.

She adjusted her cat's-eye glasses and glanced past me toward the creek bed's high willows. "Aren't you worried about your friend?"

"Not really, unless he decides to go off and hibernate with them."

"What'll he do when he's out of fish?"

I smiled. "That'll take a while."

"I can't believe we were attacked by bears."

Vic laughed, and I explained, "I don't think you were really attacked — anyway, you're in bear country, so you need to wear bear bells and carry pepper spray."

"Were those grizzlies?"

I shook my head. "No, those were black bears, but some of the old-timers say there are a few grizzlies still up here in the Bighorns."

"How do you tell the difference?"

"The scat, usually; black bears are omnivores and their scat generally has berries, nuts, foliage . . ."

"And grizzlies?"

Vic chimed in. "Their scat usually has bells in it and smells like pepper."

"Hey, can I get a hand here?"

I looked at Chuck. "I nearly forgot about you." I reached up, and, taking my hand, he jumped down to the ground and then straightened his duty belt and flat-brimmed Smokey Bear hat with a sense of self-assurance. Chuck, like me, wasn't built for running and climbing.

"Good thing you came along."

I nodded. "They probably saw your hat and thought you were one of them."

"Very funny."

I watched as the young woman walked around a bit, keeping her eyes in the direction in which the Cheyenne Nation had disappeared. I turned back to the game ranger. "What's going on, Chuck?"

He gestured toward his truck, probably anxious to get near his vehicle. "Maybe I should let her explain."

The four of us made the short walk to the half-ton and stopped by the cab to listen to Ms. Napier as she folded her arms and shuddered. "I've never seen anything like it; it just came up from underneath me in an explosion, and I ran out of there."

Vic looked between the two of them. "Wait, there was a bear in the restroom?"

The woman looked embarrassed. "I'm not sure what it was."

I gestured toward the structure. "But something attacked you in there?"

"Yes."

"Before or after the bears?"

She sighed. "I was inside, hiding from the bears, when I thought, well, you know, I'd take advantage. I've learned in Wyoming you do that 'cause you never know when you'll have the chance next."

I turned to Chuck. "And where did you come into all this?"

He reached in, turned off his light bar, and shut the door of his truck. Leaning against it, he offered the forest service water bottle to Andrea; it appeared that the two of them had gotten along in their time on the roof.

"I pulled in when I saw the bears around the toilet and got out of my vehicle just as she came blowing out the door of the convenience — scared the bears off long enough for her to get to me, but then they saw her and I guess they figured she had more caramel corn and took off after both of us." He nodded toward his vehicle. "We tried to get in here but they had gotten between us and the truck, so we had to make for the nearest building. Andrea said she wouldn't go back inside, bears or no bears, so we climbed on top."

Vic chimed in after glancing around, but we couldn't see the Bear or the bears. "I bet that was a short conversation."

The ranger looked at his wristwatch. "I

figured we were going to have to wait till the septic service got here to pump this one out for the winter — it's due in about twenty minutes or so."

The woman looked a little disgruntled. "Look, are you people going to do something about this?"

Chuck glanced at me, having the same response I normally had to people who referred to me or mine as *you people,* but then his voice became playful. "Well, the first thing I'm going to do is write you a citation for fifty dollars if this is your first offense in feeding bears, two hundred if it's your second, but if it's your third, the fine goes up to a thousand and six months of jail time." He acted as if he was going to pull out a pencil and his citation booklet. "So, which is it, first, second, or third?"

She stared at him and then smiled. "My first."

"So you saw it, whatever it was, in the restroom?"

She shook her head at me. "Not really."

"And the culprit is still in there?" I shared a look with Chuck and Vic and the three of us glanced back at the Porta Potty. "You've got it locked in the john?"

The ranger threw a thumb toward the woman. "Whatever it was, it appears to have attacked this lady in situ."

My undersheriff snickered. "You're kidding."

Andrea stepped from one foot to the next. "Look, you might think this is funny . . ." I held up a hand in my best cop manner, but she wasn't stopping. "It scratched my ass all to pieces, and I still have to go."

None of us were quite sure what to say to that, but Chuck jumped in with what he thought was the obvious. "Well, just walk over to those trees near the hillside."

"No way." She glanced at the creek and then at him as if the answer should've been obvious. "Bears."

We all turned and looked at the campground bathroom.

It was really unfair to call it a Porta Potty. It was actually much more than that — what they call in the literature a self-contained, freestanding restroom facility. It sat on a concrete pad and was made of heavy wood with a lower foundation of masonry and river rock. With a short overhang and shallow shingled roof, it must've been a chore to climb onto.

I was the most curious to see what might be in there, so I was the one elected to grip the metal handle of the forest service convenience and open the door. I'd placed an ear against it but hadn't heard anything. "Is everybody ready?"

"Wait. Where are the bears?" Andrea was standing back near Chuck's truck with the door open so she could get in quickly should the need arise.

I gestured toward the small valley leading up into the true high country. "I saw Henry a good quarter mile away leading them across the creek."

She looked unsure. "What if there's another one in there?"

I shook my head. "I don't think they would leave one behind; besides, if it was a bear we'd have heard something by now." I glanced at the building. "Whatever it is, it's not making much noise."

Chuck and I stood in front of the door as Vic stepped to the other side, reaching under her Flyers sweatshirt and drawing her sidearm from a hideout holster at her hip. When I looked at her, she shrugged. "Fuck it; we don't know what's in there."

I sighed, pulled the lever, and yanked the door wide.

Empty.

There was a large scarf lying on the concrete floor of the small structure but nothing else out of the ordinary. Vic, with the 9mm extended, moved forward and looked inside like she was part of a SWAT team. "Clear."

Chuck and I looked up and down in the confined space.

I picked up the finely made copper-colored scarf and showed it to the woman, who was still standing by Coon's truck. "This yours?"

"Yes. I'm a costumer in Los Angeles — you know, for TV and stuff. I knit it myself."

"Do you want to come and get it?"

"Not really."

I nodded and threw the thing over my shoulder as Chuck stepped closer, taking a better look around the interior of the enclosure. After a moment, I peered into the hole of the throne and gestured at his belt; when he tried to hand me his sidearm, I shook my head and pointed at the flashlight on his hip.

Coon slid the Maglite from its holder, handed it to me, and I clicked it on to shine the beam into the vault below.

An eerie sound echoed from the toilet. *"Who-who-who-whoo-whoo-whooo . . ."*

The ranger looked at me. "Owl?"

Holding the sleeve of my leather jacket under my nose, I moved the beam around carefully, finally stopping when a pair of golden eyes looked back at me.

*"Who-who-who-whoo-whoo-whooo . . ."*

Vic came up beside me and peered into the hole. "How the hell did it get in there?"

Chuck looked around the enclosure, but the windows and the door looked sound. Stepping the rest of the way out, he glanced up at the vent stack on the roof and pointed. "Through there; some owls are cavity nesters and they look for dark, confined spaces for nesting and roosting. This one must've gone in through the vent and got stuck." He sighed. "Thousands of owls die in these exact conditions. The Teton Raptor Center in Jackson has a program that puts screening over the restroom vents to keep the things from getting killed, but I guess they haven't gotten to the Bighorns yet."

The Napier woman called out from the truck. "What is it?"

"An owl."

She looked at me, a little incredulous. "In the toilet?"

"It would appear."

"Well, can you get it out?"

I shined the Maglite back into the vault. "My arms aren't long enough."

I glanced at Vic, but she shook her head. "If you can't reach him, there's no way I can."

Coon glanced at his wristwatch again. "The honey wagon is going to be here anytime now." He stepped outside and fetched a large rock to prop open the restroom door. "Sorry, I can't take the smell."

"What will they do?"

"They'll pump the thing out."

"With the owl in there."

"Yeah." He glanced through the open doorway. "The only thing they could do is pump it there on the ground." He made a face. "But I'm not telling them to do that in a national forest; besides, the bird wouldn't make it anyway."

Andrea had crept closer — I guess she decided that danger from the owl wasn't imminent. "Look, I'm going to get out of here and go find another toilet, but I have no idea where there is one. Can somebody show me?"

Chuck paused for a moment and then shrugged. "Duty calls."

"You're leaving?"

He started toward his truck. "I'll run her down to Lost Cabin Campground and then I'll try and come back, okay?"

"Motherfucker." Vic looked at me as the ranger turned his truck around, and Ms. Napier followed him up the road in her vehicle. "How about a stick?"

I sighed and walked toward the barrow ditch, found a likely limb about as big around as one of my fingers, and returned to the restroom. I leaned over the toilet and gingerly poked the stick down into the vault, careful to avoid the livid, round, iridescent eyes that continued to watch my every move.

Heck, I'd be angry stuck in there, too.

I adjusted the stick and slowly brought it over to where I thought the owl was, felt a brief tug, and then heard a sharp snap. Feeling nothing more, I pulled it out and looked at the broken end. "Yikes."

Vic peered into the darkness of the vault. "I'm not sticking my hand or anything else in there where that damn thing can get at it."

I turned to see the Cheyenne Nation approaching from the willows near the creek with the now-empty plastic tray in his hand. "What is going on?"

"There's an owl in there."

He tossed the tray onto the hood of his truck and continued toward us. "What kind?"

"An angry one." Vic looked past him. "Where are the bears?"

"Up the creek; I took them past where the

water is more swift and then climbed across on a fallen tree. I do not think they will go to the trouble of doubling back — they are pretty full of fish."

I glanced in the hole. "We're trying to figure out how to get him out of here."

He looked at my shoulder. "Nice scarf." I'd forgotten to give the costumer back her accessory.

*"Who-who-who-whoo-whoo-whooo . . ."*

Henry leaned over the throne, and I clicked on the Maglite to give him a clearer view. He breathed out a breath through puckered lips. "Whew . . . great horned owl, princess of the Camp of the Dead."

"Princess?"

He nodded. "It is a juvenile female."

Vic leaned in. "Now how the hell do you know that?"

The Cheyenne Nation smiled. "The call, it is distinctively feminine."

My undersheriff shook her head. "Distinctively screwed is what she is."

Henry looked at me, and I filled him in. "The sewage people are going to be here any minute, and they're going to pump the vault out, owl and all."

The Bear straightened in a manner not unlike the other bear on-the-fight that we'd just confronted. "You cannot do that."

233

"Henry . . ."

"This may not simply be an owl."

I shook my head at the ridiculousness of the situation. "Henry, nobody wants to see this owl killed, but . . ."

"She may be a Messenger from the Camp of the Dead, but she may be something else as well." He took a deep breath and tried to explain. "Within my nation, certain people, both male and female, who practice Medicine are believed to have the ability to shape-shift. The form they choose most is that of an owl, so that they can move silently through the night and cast spells on people while they are asleep, and at their most vulnerable to spiritual forces."

Vic looked at the Bear, then at me, and then back to the big Cheyenne. "If that's the way you're trying to convince us to save her, it isn't working."

"Among my people there is only one owl even considered to be a bird and that is the short-eared one or snake-eating owl, an important source of medicinal power for shamans." He pointed toward the toilet. "But this is not that type of owl, so it is a *Mista,* or a spirit-of-the-night. Even the *Hohnuhke,* the Cheyenne Contraries of the buffalo days, wore the feathers of the owl but never that of the great horned or the screech — their power is too strong. So it was lesser feathers that were attached to the warrior's shield, lance, or headdress to protect him, help him to see in the dark, and make him deadly silent."

Vic shrugged. "Well, this one's going to be silent and deadly here in a few minutes."

Henry held up a hand. "I am not a shaman and cannot tell the difference between the Messenger and an ordinary owl, but the holy men and women frequently seek spiritual help from these owls in conjunction with healing practices. It is believed that the owl has medicinal powers, soft and gentle, similar to its feathers."

I held up the stick and showed him the broken end. "Soft and gentle? She did this."

He shook his head in dismissal. "This is a young great horned owl and most likely the spirit of a transformed holy person, the unquiet dead. The tufts on their heads are symbolic of horns, the signs of spiritual beings like the chiefs of the underworld." He glanced at me as if there were more, more that he did not want to say. "Or, it is possible this owl is something else."

"What?"

"Being as young as she is . . ."

"What?"

He sighed and looked directly at me. "The

Spirit Messenger of an unborn soul, the herald of a young one who has yet to enter this world."

I thought about Cady. "You can't be serious."

"I am."

Vic folded her arms and leaned against the inside wall. "Oh, now, for fuck's sake."

His face was still in all seriousness. "In my belief this *Mista* or *Hiha'n Winu'cala* is the spirit of . . ."

I could feel a shudder run through me, and I thought about the prophecies that Virgil White Buffalo, the last shaman I had encountered in these mountains, had made concerning my daughter and granddaughter. "My granddaughter."

"Lola?" Vic ventured.

"Exactly."

I looked at the two of them. "We have to save this owl."

Vic stared back at me. "Have you lost your mind?"

"Maybe, but we have to save this owl."

She shot a look up at the Bear. "Look, no offense, Henry . . ." His eyes clicked to mine. "If you believe this mumbo jumbo that's fine, but I don't see how we're going to do it before the shit wagon gets here."

I reached over and lifted the lid — the

diameter of the formed plastic opening was about eighteen inches across at the widest part from front to back. "We have to try and get in there."

She made a face. "And then what?"

I pulled the copper-colored scarf from my shoulders. "We can use this to wrap around her so that she doesn't attack and then scoop her out." Ignoring the smell, I stooped by the toilet and reached in with both arms, my progress impeded where the width of my shoulders lodged against the edge of the plastic sides. "Unh-uh." I looked up at the Cheyenne Nation, but knew his shoulders were every bit as large as my own; then the two of us looked at Victoria Moretti.

She didn't move. "No fucking way."

"We can grab you by your ankles —"

"And kiss my ass! There's no way I'm crawling into that thing."

Henry leaned forward to get her attention, demonstrating the technique by raising his arms in a diving position. "If you raise your arms . . ." He demonstrated. "It will narrow your shoulder width, and we can lower you in."

She went so far as to rest her hand on her high-riding sidearm. "I'm not toilet diving for an owl."

I stood and gestured toward both Henry

and me. "We don't fit."

"Yeah, well, I don't give a rat's ass."

I placed an arm across the open doorway. "With both of us holding on to you, there's no way anything can happen."

She folded her arms. "I'm not climbing in that toilet." Her eyes flicked between us, and I could tell she was weakening, probably thinking of the things Virgil had said. She took a deep breath, gagging a little at the smell, and began unbuckling her belt. She unclipped her holstered Glock and lowered it to the ground, and began pulling her iPod, pens, notepads, keys, sunglasses, and other assorted items from her pockets and handing them to Henry and me. Pausing in the action, she shot a finger at the two of us. "You drop me, and we're all three going to be in a world of shit."

"What do you weigh, Vic?"

"Fuck you, that's what I weigh."

I glanced at the Cheyenne Nation and he nodded, both of us figuring we could lift her all day without any problems. I handed Vic the scarf, which was made of surprisingly thick yarn. "I'd wrap this around the owl as quickly as I could just to make sure she doesn't get at you."

She pulled on the gloves she'd retrieved

from Rezdawg, a wise precaution. "You're damn right."

Henry glanced into the hole and then stooped to pick Vic's sunglasses from her pile. "You might want to wear these."

She looked at the Bear. "That is a pair of two-hundred-and-twenty-dollar Oakley Fast Jacket sunglasses, and I am not about to lose them in there — anyway, don't you think it's going to be dark enough?"

Henry unfolded the expensive eyewear. "I would want some eye protection, if I were you."

Vic took the sunglasses and reluctantly put them on. "If I drop them, I'm going to want to fish them out."

The Bear nodded. "Deal."

Vic walked over and stood in front of the toilet, and I clicked on the flashlight to check on the location of the owl — she hadn't moved. "You want me to try and hold this while . . . ?"

Her voice went up a few octaves in response. "You fucking well better hold on to me; I don't want you assholes concentrating on anything other than hanging on to my legs and not letting go!"

"Right."

She glanced up at me. "I'm serious."

"I can tell." I looked at the hole and

added, "I would be, too."

She stared into the abyss. "I can't believe I'm doing this"

"It is for a greater cause." Henry placed a hand on her shoulder. "I would also keep my mouth closed."

Vic looked at him, smiled a fake smile, reached over, and unrolled a few sections of toilet paper, twisting them into impromptu nose plugs, and stuffing them into her nostrils; then she held her hands up and wrapped the scarf between both of them. "Ready."

Henry and I reached down and gripped her legs at the knees and ankles. We easily lifted her and flipped her over. "You okay?"

She nodded, and we began lowering her into the vault, outstretched arms and the scarf first. There was a fluttering noise, and Vic struggled, but our grip remained firm. "What's happening?"

Her voice, muffled and nasal, echoed up from the chamber. "She's moved over to the other side. Can you turn me so I'm facing her more?"

The Bear and I looked at each other, trying to imagine how we were going to accomplish that; finally Henry straddled the back of the toilet and stepped over as I pivoted to the right. "That better?"

There was another fluttering from below, and Vic's voice sounded against the concrete that was underneath the floor. "I think. It's so dark down here and with the glasses, I can't see anything." There was a pause, and then she spoke again. "You're going to have to lower me more; I can't reach into the corner where I think she is."

"How much?"

The voice echoed up. "Maybe another foot — but no more than that."

Henry and I started lowering her when she called out, "Stop!"

"Right."

"It's going to take me a minute to get ready, so just hold me here."

The Cheyenne Nation and I stood over the toilet with Vic Moretti's feet in our faces, and I thought that even her feet smelled nice, but maybe it was just compared to the environs. There wasn't much else to do, so I broached the subject again. "Lola?"

He nodded with a sense of finality, the kind of finality that usually meant The Greatest Legal Mind of Our Time had made up her mind. "Lola, short for Dolores, taken from the title of the Virgin Mary: Virgen Maria de los Dolores."

"Our Lady of Sorrows?"

He thought about it. "Well, yes . . . technically."

Vic's voice echoed up again. "Great, that can be her stage name."

He shook his head at me, and we felt Vic move in our hands again, probably preparing for the monumental grab. "You still okay?"

"Hang on — this might get a little hairy here in a second."

I gripped my undersheriff's leg a little tighter. Henry grunted. I looked up at him. "What?"

His dark eyes rested easy on mine. "What what?"

"You said something?"

"No."

I shrugged but then heard the grunt again, this time while looking directly at his face — his mouth hadn't moved. Both of us looked at each other with eyebrows raised before pivoting our heads in unison toward the propped open door of the restroom where the sow black bear was sniffing the ground just off the concrete pad. "Vic . . ."

"Hold it steady, I'm making my move . . ."

The black bear raised her head up and looked into the restroom at the sound of my voice. You really don't get a sense of how big the things are until you're up close and personal with them. The sow was roughly our height, but the months of summer bounty had helped her to pack on the weight, and I was betting she weighed well more than Henry and me together. Their eyesight isn't the greatest, but their sense of smell is extremely acute and the things that repulse us smell like the Usual at the Busy Bee Café to them.

I spoke sotto voce. "I thought you said they wouldn't double back?"

The Bear's whisper was low and steady. "They did not, but evidently she did."

"I think we should pull Vic out."

"I agree."

We were about to do that when Vic made her move, a jarring lunge that made for a mad fluttering and some vicious swearing along with a certain amount of animation translating up her legs to us.

The sow huffed a few breaths and then moved as she'd done when we first pulled up in Rezdawg — she bounced twice and stood up to her full height, the bunching of muscle mass in her shoulders threatening without so much as a gesture. I'd heard it said that the beasts were about six times as powerful as a man, and looking at the sheer girth of her, I didn't have many doubts. Henry and I were outmanned by four —

well, three-and-a-half, counting Vic.

She sniffed the air again and peered into the semidarkness of the enclosure, perhaps four yards away from us.

I spoke as quietly as I could. "Henry?"

"Do not move."

Vic's voice rose again at our boots, a little more frantic this time. "I've got her! I've got her! Pull me up before she gets away, damn it!"

I figured I could get at my sidearm, even holding Vic, since I had Henry's help, even if all I wanted to do was fire off a warning shot. The bear cocked her head like a dog, and all I could think was that as horrible as Vic's predicament was, she was the one most likely to survive this situation without getting mauled.

Vic kicked a little. "Hey, get me the hell out of here!"

The bear took a step toward us, still sniffing the air.

I spoke through the side of my mouth. "Vic, stop kicking and . . ."

"What? Hey, this bitch bird is sinking its claws into my boobs!"

The sow took another step toward us, chuffing and ducking her head down like she might charge.

The Bear's voice remained calm. "She will

bluff at least once, maybe twice, before she really charges, if she does."

"Ouch, damn it! This isn't funny!"

I continued speaking out of the side of my mouth. "Do you think if she realizes there are three of us, she might back down?"

"That or we can feed her Vic."

The sow lunged forward, even going so far as to swipe one of the support poles at the edge of the pad, which sent a shudder through the structure. At the same time, we yanked as hard as we could, sending my undersheriff up and out of the hole. The bundle she was carrying exploded in a flurry of copper yarn and wing flapping as the great horned owl wasted no time in freeing herself, sending Vic to the floor and the two of us against the walls.

Up close, she was an amazing thing to see — the radiating feathers splayed out like a serrated sunburst, and even though she was only an adolescent, her wings seemed to fill the room. Three powerful swoops, and she levitated and blew out the open door straight into the bear.

It was as if Henry's prophecies had come true; a possessed soul of the underworld had risen from the depth with all the fury of a feathered banshee.

The sow didn't know what hit her, and

she didn't care; as soon as the owl started out, the bear beat a hasty retreat as fast as her four legs could carry her. The last we saw she was headed through the red willow thickets and back up the valley.

We all lay there in the aftermath, Vic looking like she'd had the worst of it, her face still red from hanging upside down for so long. "What the hell just happened?"

I looked through the open doorway and could see the scarf reflecting copper on the ground between us and Henry's truck, but there was no sign of the owl; it was as if she had simply disappeared.

I glanced at the Cheyenne Nation, and watched as he walked out of the structure and kneeled in the gravel out front, carefully picking up an elongated brown and white feather, rolling the quill of it between thumb and forefinger. "I think we just witnessed the *Mista.*"

Vic felt her head, glanced around on the floor, and then looked back at the toilet. "I think I dropped my sunglasses."

Coasting to let Rezdawg's brakes cool on the slow drive down the mountain, Henry and I discussed the finer points of what had happened and their exact meanings. Vic ignored us and continued listening to her music.

"So, you think the owl was there to save us?"

"I do."

"And that it was a herald of my grand-daughter?"

"Possibly." He nodded curtly, as if the question was settled. "It is its connection with death, the afterlife, and rebirth that marks the owl as an embodiment of spirits; I think she was the herald at the fork of the Hanging Road, the Milky Way, which leads to the Camp of the Dead. She has the power to decide who shall pass and who will be stillborn or condemned to wander the earth as spirits or *wana'gi* forever. The *Hiha'n Winu'cala* is responsible for this transition, and you must cry your name to her so she can assess the merit of your attached soul. If you have a good name, you may pass the junction of the fork, but if your name is bad, you are shunted onto a dead-end branch."

Vic, her ear buds back in and her eyes closed, continued to ignore us, and I leaned a little forward so that I could see the Bear. "So, according to Cheyenne beliefs you have a name before you arrive in this world?"

"Yes. We always have a name, both before and after our time here."

"Can you change your name?"

He nodded. "Yes, but you risk changing your path, and the *Mista* may deny you."

"You mean not let you in or out of the world?"

"Yes. It can be complicated." He sighed as he pulled back out onto the main road in a low gear, lugging Rezdawg down the mountain as his fingers came up to stroke the feather, now hanging from his rearview mirror along with his medicine bag. "My father lived with death for a very long time, and I remember the night he died a great horned owl was sitting on the poles of our family teepee outside the house. When I would go and visit his grave, there was always an owl feather there and still is today."

I was about to say something more when Vic, who had adjusted her iPod, leaned forward and began drumming on the dash very softly.

*Lola, Lo-lo-lo-lo-Lola . . .*

Lola.

# PETUNIA, BANDIT QUEEN OF THE BIGHORNS

Static. "He's disconsolate and won't stop crying."

I stared at the radio under my dash and then keyed the mic. "So, what do you want us to do about it?"

Static. "Well, you're the one with the Basque deputy."

"The guy's Basque?"

Static. "Yeah."

I tried not to get involved with the national forest service, the rangers, or anything happening in the federal jurisdiction when I didn't have to, but it was looking more and more like I was going to have to, and as usual it would be Chuck Coon who got me into it.

I keyed the mic and peeked at Dog in the rearview mirror. "Well, fortunately for you I've got two of my faithful companions with me." I glanced over at Santiago Saizarbitoria. "You up for it?"

The dark-eyed young man looked out at the Bighorn Mountain scenery speeding by under the clear blue sky of the stunning spring afternoon. "Sure."

"What's the Basque phrase for people who leave their country?" I steered the Bullet past Crazy Woman Canyon and took the Hazelton Road south toward Upper Doyle Creek where the grazing land adjoined the property owned by the feds. Sancho's wife, Maria, and son, Antonio, were visiting family down in Rawlins, and I got the idea that he was missing them more than he wanted to let on. "You don't seem really enthused."

He chose his next words carefully, not being a big one for airing his slightly soiled laundry with his coworkers. "When she was alive . . . I mean, did you and your wife fight a lot?"

"Sometimes." I glanced at him. "You and Maria?"

"Yeah."

"About what?"

He blew his breath out between his teeth. "She got a dog."

I glanced in the rearview mirror at the beast in the back. "I thought you liked dogs."

"I do, but she went to the pound and got a border collie–blue heeler puppy, and you know how they are if you don't have something for them to do."

I grunted. "You got any furniture left?"

"A few sticks, but he's turned his attention to the woodwork in the rented house and it's taking a beating." Sancho gazed out the window and dropped the Basque term for their expatriates. *"Diaspora."*

"That's it." I watched him for a while longer. "You thinking about running away and becoming a shepherd?" He didn't laugh, and I figured that maybe I better redirect the conversation. "You know the government effectively cut off immigration to Basques in 1921 with the National Origins Quota Act."

"And why did they do that?"

I shrugged. "Too many Basques, I guess — and you know what that leads to."

His eyes shifted toward me. "What?"

"Harmonized singing, synchronized dancing, drinking, and general joyous humanity."

He bent his mouth in a tight-lipped smile. "Well, we don't want that, do we?"

"Nope, but a senator over in Nevada, McCarran, opened it back up with the Immigration Act of 1952, allowing a quota of five hundred for Spanish sheepherders — I wonder what he had against the French." I pulled the truck off the gravel road through an open gate onto the sparse two-track, then slid to a stop and reached back to scratch the fur behind Dog's ears. "Of course now they enter the country under the H-2A temporary agricultural workers program that lets companies hire foreigners for jobs Americans won't do. Much more pedantic sounding."

"Do you really sit around and memorize that stuff?" He looked at me, unsure as to why I'd stopped the truck.

"Would you get out and shut that gate? Evidently Ranger Coon wasn't brought up in a ranching family."

He did as I asked, then hopped back in. I pulled out, lecturing him a little more on his culture. "You know those guys have one of the highest suicide rates of any occupation, right?"

"Senators?"

"Shepherds."

He continued to stare at the lonely hills still wearing a dusting of early spring snow.

Thinking I could get him to feel better about his own situation, I continued. "The poor *borregueros* are out here in the middle of nowhere most of the year, getting paid $650 a month, living in a five-foot-by-ten-foot camper without running water, a toilet, or electricity . . ." I took a breath. "I'd imagine it gets tough."

We drove along, and he still said nothing.

"It borders on total social isolation."

Finally, he pulled the bill of his ball cap over his eyes and leaned back in his seat. "Sounds pretty good to me right now."

We pulled to a stop near a stand of lodgepole pines beside Coon's mint-green forest service Jeep. Looking through the windshield of my truck, I could see a battered sheep wagon, a sad-looking sorrel gelding, about a hundred sheep, and the gray-shirted ranger standing over a man with his face in his hands and a bolt-action .22 lying across his thighs.

Thinking it best not to tempt Dog with the hundred sheep, we cracked the window and left him in the truck and approached the two men. Coon waved and stepped aside, happy to hand over the sensitive situation. The sheepherder looked young, but the burnished skin of his hands and face bore testament to many an hour spent out in the elements.

Santiago stepped ahead of me and kneeled down to the man seated on the steps of the wagon, gently took the rifle away, and handed it to me; I pulled the bolt action and caught the diminutive round as it popped out.

*"Kaixo."*

The man had been crying and wiped the remainder of his tears away with the sleeve of his shirt as Saizarbitoria bumped the suntanned man's shoulder with the back of his hand in a comradely manner to get his attention. *"Pozten nair zu ezagutzeaz. Zer moduz?"* The man didn't respond and sat there looking at him blankly. *"Nola duzu izena?"*

Finally, the man grunted a response. *"Qué?"*

Sancho stared at him. *"Barkatu . . . Ba al dakizueuskaraz?"*

He shook his head. *"Qué?"*

The Basquo's face dropped into the palm of one hand, the next words mumbled through his fingers. *"Hablas español?"*

The man immediately straightened and smiled. *"Sí!"* Rattling off a monologue far faster than I could understand with my high school Spanish, he and Sancho talked for a while.

In a lull, my deputy glanced up. "His name is José Vargas, and he's from Chile."

We both looked at Coon, who folded his arms. "Well, I didn't know what he was talking about — he's in a sheep wagon and

herding sheep, so I figured he was Basque."
At a loss for anything else to say, he changed
tack. "When I pulled up here, he was sitting
there crying, and I couldn't get out of him
what the problem was so I called you guys."

I glanced at the man and then to Saizarbitoria. "Did he tell you what was the matter?"

There was another flurry of Spanish as
the swarthy man gestured toward an older
sheep with a unique fleece that we hadn't
noticed before tied to the wheel of the
wagon, a lamb staying nearby.

The Basquo listened intently, hiding a grin
and trying to repress the humor of the situation, finally standing and placing his hands
on his hips and looking at us. "Evidently,
we are in the presence of royalty."

Coon looked down at the sad man. "What,
he's the prince of Chile?"

"If my translation is on the mark, it's not
him." Saizarbitoria smiled and swept off his
hat in mock respect, gesturing toward the
sheep tied to the wagon who now bleated at
us. "It's her." He laughed. "Gentlemen, may
I introduce Petunia, Bandit Queen of the
Bighorns."

The ranger was the first to respond.
"You're shitting me. That's the ewe that
launched a thousand strays?"

I glanced past the men at the sheep with the florid fleece. "Well, I'll be."

Sancho looked at all three of us as if we were crazy. "If it's not too much to ask, who the hell is Petunia, Bandit Queen of the Bighorns?"

The saga was an odd one in the storied past of Sheridan, Big Horn, Washakie, and Absaroka Counties, a detailed tale that I'd heard from Vic Garber, the original and present owner of Petunia, and I told it as best I knew.

"When you are running flocks as large as a couple thousand on rough range, you have to have what they call in the business 'markers.' So that the herders can get a rough count, you have one for each hundred head of stock. Well, about five years ago on the Garber ranch near Sheridan, a ewe foaled a lamb with a somewhat unique wool pattern that for all intents and purposes resembled a flowering petunia — hence, the legend was born."

Saizarbitoria waited patiently and then looked at me dubiously. "She's famous in four counties because she looks like a petunia?"

"Petunia and her mother went to summer pasture in the mountains and then returned to the Garber place, and since Petunia was a good-sized ewe and had a distinctive pattern, Garber kept her as a marker. Paul Miller was Vic's top herder at that time, and he made sure that Petunia, being such a stunning sheep, was bred. She had a lamb, although not one as distinctive as she was. Well, as these things sometimes happen with cattle or sheep, Petunia hated her lamb, so she was given the usual treatment until she accepted the baby. She went up to the Bighorns that summer with her lamb and things were fine."

I paused to catch my breath. "Well, the second year Miller bred Petunia, she had her lamb and loved it, so was sent to the mountains again. Along toward the end of August, Garber was up checking on his camp when Paul told him that Petunia was gone a couple of nights that week, but was back now. Garber, a tough old hand and a shrewd businessman, knew that a rogue sheep could lead a lot of the others astray, so he told Miller that if she was a bunch-quitter, to shoot her."

Saizarbitoria looked at me in horror. "Shoot the sheep?"

I nodded my head. "Miller pretty much had the same response and said, 'Oh, I couldn't do that, what about the lamb?' Garber knew that Miller and the flock of sheep were up there at around nine or ten thousand feet, so he tells him to butcher the lamb and to stick what he can't eat into a snowbank and says he'll take the rest home the next time he comes up."

Sancho glanced at Coon. "He killed the lamb?"

Chuck shook his head. "I haven't ever heard the whole story."

They both turned back to me, and I stuffed my hands into my jeans. "Well, the next time Garber goes up there, Paul tells him that before he could shoot her, Petunia lit out and that she had taken a bunch of sheep with her when she left. So Garber tells him that the next time he sees her, he's to shoot the damn sheep on sight. Well, Miller doesn't want to do it, but Garber tells him that they'll lose the whole flock before she's through, so shoot her."

It was possible that the Chilean shepherd, Vargas, knew a little English, because he was now listening intently.

"Vic gets home that night and Tom Koltiska from down here in Absaroka County calls him up and tells him that he's got a sheep with Garber's brand on it, a marker with an unusual pattern in her wool and that he's at a loss to describe it. Whereupon Garber mutters into the phone, 'Petunia.'

"Tom yells, 'That's her!' "

Coon began laughing.

"Garber tells him, 'Tom, do me a favor and shoot her.' Well, Tom tells him that he doesn't want to do that and says, 'What about the lamb?' Garber tells him to butcher the lamb and to have dinner on him, but Tom says that he hates the thought and, by the way, she came with more than a truckload of Garber's outlaw strays. So, they make arrangements for him to go down there and pick them up, Garber thinking that he would take Petunia's fate into his own hands. He is there the next morning bright and early, but the first thing Tom says is that Petunia's gone again but not to worry because she and her lamb are on Chip Lawrence's place near Ten Sleep and they'll bring her over at noon."

Saizarbitoria shook his head. "That's over sixty miles."

"The pickup shows at around twelve, and Garber says he can tell by the way the guys are behaving that they're a little apprehensive. The foreman comes over and introduces himself and tells Vic that that damned marker of his must have a sixth sense and has gotten away again."

Chuck was still laughing.

"Garber tells 'em that if they ever lay eyes

on her that they are to shoot her on sight, but the head guy says that he doesn't want to do that. Vic tells him that that damned sheep has already gotten three different ranchers in trouble, so shoot her. Well, the men ask about the lamb, and Garber tells 'em to eat it."

"Later that year in December, Tommy Wayman and one of his men were rewiring some of their sheds over in Big Horn County up near Shell and guess who shows up?"

Sancho asked. "Did they call Garber?"

"They did."

"And she got away again?"

"Yep." I glanced past the men at the sheep, who was looking innocent enough tied to the wagon wheel with her lamb nearby. "Gentlemen, in six years that sheep has covered the entire Bighorn Mountain range who knows how many times."

We all had a laugh, and then the Basquo glanced down at José and rattled off a few words of Spanish. The shepherd responded, and then his eyes welled up again. Sancho smiled and patted the man's shoulder. "He says he radioed in to the rancher who contacted Garber and . . . Well, you can guess what the verdict is."

I looked at the .22 in my hands, thinking

about the plan that I had just formulated and how I was going to play this.

José spoke some more, and Sancho translated. "He says that all the shepherds on the mountain know her and love her, that she's a legend and he doesn't want to be the one to do it."

I glanced at Coon, but he backed away. "Oh, no . . . Not me — not my responsibility."

Carefully returning the small round into the bolt-action, I slid the mechanism home and stood there like Tom Horn, judge and executioner, aware that if I overdid it I was going to have to shoot a sheep and worse, her lamb.

"No, boss, really?"

I spoke with my most resolute voice. "It's got to be done — she's costing these ranchers money and time that they don't have."

Putting on my most reluctant performance, I started to walk around him, but he held up an arm. "What about the lamb?"

"It'll have to go, too." I gestured toward Vargas and walked the fine line of overkill. "Ask him if he's got any more ammunition for the .22 — I'd hate to use my .45 on a lamb."

Saizarbitoria stood there, looking at me.

■ ■ ■ ■

It didn't take long for Chuck and me to safely tie both Petunia and her lamb to the hold-down eyelets in the bed of my truck as the Basquo carried on a conversation with the shepherd and then joined us at the Bullet. "He says he won't take any money, but I'll just run him up some groceries and a bottle of red wine next week."

Chuck looked at him. "You'd better keep the Bandit Queen locked up tight, or every rancher in Wyoming is going to be after you — especially Garber."

Santiago walked over to the truck and pulled the wool back away from the sheep's eyes, and I could pretty well figure that there was some kind of connection going on between the aged ewe and the genetic coding in the Basquo. "Maybe her wandering days are over; we've got almost an acre behind the house that's fenced."

Saizarbitoria and I climbed into the Bullet and waved good-bye, turning back onto the dirt two-track, slowly descending out of the high pasture. Sancho threw an arm over the seat and looked past Dog into the bed. "At least that damned puppy of ours will have something to do now."

I drove the entire forty miles without cracking a smile — a personal best.

The employees of Thorndike Press hope you have enjoyed this Large Print book. All our Thorndike, Wheeler, and Kennebec Large Print titles are designed for easy reading, and all our books are made to last. Other Thorndike Press Large Print books are available at your library, through selected bookstores, or directly from us.

For information about titles, please call:
  (800) 223-1244

or visit our Web site at:
  http://gale.cengage.com/thorndike

To share your comments, please write:
  Publisher
  Thorndike Press
  10 Water St., Suite 310
  Waterville, ME 04901